AUSTRALIAN NURSE

Verity's favourite patient told her that she reminded him of a lady in a poem, so easily made glad. He thought it a lovely quality, but she was soon reflecting bitterly that he was all too right. She had been warned against that high-powered charmer, Dr. Webber, but had given her heart away recklessly and without reserve, and then had been left wondering if she had imagined something that did not exist.

HARRIET SMITH

◆

AUSTRALIAN NURSE

Complete and Unabridged

LINFORD
Leicester

First published in Great Britain in 1980 by
Robert Hale Limited
London

First Linford Edition
published 1997
by arrangement with
Robert Hale Limited
London

British Library CIP Data

Smith, Harriet
  Australian nurse.—Large print ed.—
Linford romance library
  1. Love stories 2. Large type books
  I. Title
  823.9'14 [F]

ISBN 0–7089–5180–5

Published by
F. A. Thorpe (Publishing) Ltd.
Anstey, Leicestershire

Set by Words & Graphics Ltd.
Anstey, Leicestershire
Printed and bound in Great Britain by
T. J. International Ltd., Padstow, Cornwall

This book is printed on acid-free paper

1

EVEN in Paris, a grey, soaking wet day does nothing for a girl's looks. It was the more surprising that, on this wet day, a comparatively plain girl should catch and hold the eyes of a good-looking young man in their party. Her prettier companion was becoming increasingly disgruntled as the rain continued to pour down, but Verity's enthusiasm sparkled undamped, and the gaiety of her smile brightened the greyness. The young man edged nearer, listening to their conversation, He then asked.

"Are you from Australia, or New Zealand?"

Verity turned, amusement in her eyes. "I suppose that's our accent. We're Australians, and some people seem to think it awful. You're English?"

"Yes, from the West Country."

1

"The West Country!" Her eyes sparkled with interest. "Two of my grandparents came from there, though I'm not sure which part, so I want to go there before I go home. I'm only spending a year in England, less if I can't get a job, and we left the plane at Rome, so that we could see a little of Italy and France as well."

They were on a sight-seeing tour of Paris, and after this introduction, they finished the tour as a trio.

"Shall we go and get some tea, after all this wet sight-seeing?" the newcomer suggested eventually.

"Tea in Paris is much too expensive," Verity objected.

"You can please yourself, but I'm having a cup of tea, whatever it costs," declared her companion. She cast an appraising eye over the young man, and decided to accept his company. "I'm Amanda Robins, and this is Verity Lawson."

"And I'm Ralph Blake."

They found a café, and Verity, a little

reluctantly, joined them in the extravagance of tea.

"Amanda can afford to be a bit of a spendthrift, because she's got a job fixed up in Oxford," she explained. "But I joined her at short notice, and have no job to go to, so I've got to be careful. I don't know how long it will take me to find a job, or if my money will last out."

With their wet hoods removed, Amanda was revealed as a pretty, fair-haired girl of twenty-five. Verity was only twenty, medium height and slightly built, with undistinguished features, except for a pair of really beautiful hazel eyes. Ralph looked somewhere in his early twenties, with a sunburnt face, thick fair hair that waved untidily, and a good-natured, easy-going manner. Their tongues wagged freely over the tea, the two girls talking about places they had seen, while Ralph told them that he had been camping with friends in Provence, but had to return home before the others, so decided to spend a couple of days seeing Paris.

"What sort of work do you want in England?" he asked.

"We're both nurses," Verity told him. "Amanda has got a job in an Oxford hospital, because her married sister is living there. I'm only part-trained. so I'm not sure what kind of job I can get. I meant to finish my training, then come, but things were difficult at home, and Amanda was coming, so I just decided to join her at short notice. What I'd like is several temporary jobs, in different parts of the country, with sight-seeing holidays in between, and I don't really mind what I do; nursing for preference, but I'd be an au pair, or a mother's help, or almost anything."

"You could have got a temporary job in a holiday resort, if you'd come earlier," said Ralph. "But they're un-likely to be taking on extra staff in late August. How long are you staying in Paris?"

4

"Only for one more day."

"Then flying to London?"

"No, we come from an inland town, and thought a sea crossing would be more of a change."

"I'm going back the same day," Ralph informed them "so you could come in my car, and save the train fare."

The two girls glanced at one another, then decided to accept this handsome offer.

"What are you doing tomorrow?" Ralph asked.

"Shopping," said Amanda. "The Louvre," answered Verity at the same moment. "We could shop in the morning, and go round the gallery in the afternoon," she added.

"After a morning round the shops, I'd rather have something easier on the feet," retorted Amanda.

"I'm going on a river cruise, so why not join me?" Ralph suggested. He pulled a leaflet from his pocket, marked the trip he intended to go on, and gave it to them. Then they exchanged hotel addresses, in case they did not meet again, and Ralph told them what time he would call for them, for the journey to England.

After a morning's shopping, nearly all of it Amanda's, Verity again hopefully suggested the Louvre for the afternoon, but Amanda again declined, very firmly.

"I've been round enough art galleries with you to last me for a whole year, at least," she insisted. "You must do as you please, but I think I shall go on that river cruise. It's just the afternoon for it."

Verity sighed, but eventually she agreed to go with Amanda, and enjoyed the trip as thoroughly as she enjoyed most things.

"Would you consider a job in an old people's home?" Ralph asked her, while they consumed ice-cream in a riverside garden.

"I'd like it, provided it was a good place," she said slowly. "Why? Do you know of a job in one?"

"Not exactly. I have an aunt, a great-aunt to be exact, who is living in a nursing-home, about seven miles from my own town, Bretton. That's in Somerset, and it occurred to me that you might be interested, as you want to see the West Country. I can't guarantee that there'd be a job for you, but I do know they always seem to be short of staff, and Aunt Janet frequently complains about the service. All the same, it must be a good place, or she wouldn't stay. I believe they take a few disabled people, and short-stay convalescents, but it's mostly old people. If you're interested, you could drive down there tomorrow with me, and I'll ask Matron about a job. She knows me, which could be a help. Even if there's nothing for you, you could have a look round the West Country, and perhaps find a different job there."

Verity considered Ralph thoughtfully. He had a pleasant, open, boyish expression. She liked him, and was flattered that he liked her. "I'm certainly interested," she admitted, "and it's kind of you to suggest it. I'd like to think it over, if I could let you know tomorrow?"

"Just as you like. You'd enjoy the drive down there, and you could look up your West Country origins. Did your forbears come from an old family, some historic manor house?"

"Now, you're laughing at me," said Verity unresentfully. "I'm sure they didn't, though they might have been servants, or farm workers at some such place. Perhaps not, though. Gran had had a good education. Grandfather's people might have been small trades-men, or something like that. He was bright enough up top, but hopeless with his hands, broke everything he touched! Someone descended from farm workers would probably inherit skilful hands."

"It doesn't follow. The skill might have skipped a generation," put in Amanda. "You have the neatest fingers I have ever known, for most things,

8

nursing, sewing, painting."

"Do you paint?" asked Ralph. "Is that why you're so interested in art galleries?"

"I do a bit, but only for fun." On an impulse, Verity took out the boat leaflet he had given her. There was a blank page at the back, and on this she drew a quick sketch of Ralph's profile. In spite of the speed, it was a good likeness, and he looked very impressed.

"If you can make a sketch like this in a few minutes, you could surely do something really good, if you took your time?"

"It might be better, or it might be much worse," she laughed. "My drawings can be pretty hit or miss, and I never know which they'll be until they're done."

"Well, I shall certainly keep this."

They returned to the boat, had a meal together at the end of the trip, and then the two girls returned to their hotel to pack, as they were making an early start, next morning.

"Do you intend to go to the West

Country, with Ralph?" asked Amanda.

"I don't know, but it's very tempting," mused Verity. "I want to see that part of the country, and I want to get a job as soon as possible."

"You've no guarantee of a job. I think you'd do better to come to Oxford with me, as you planned. There must be plenty of university staff who want au pair girls, even if you can't find a nursing job. It would be quite a long drive, alone with a man you know nothing about."

"I like him, and I think he was just trying to help. I'm grateful."

"He may have reasons of his own for suggesting the job."

"Such as what?" asked Verity derisively.

Amanda didn't try to answer this. "I wouldn't fancy a job like that," she said instead. "You'd get very little real nursing. Most of your time would be spent waiting on a lot of pampered, rich old people. You heard what Ralph said about his aunt always complaining about the service."

"Even rich old people need someone to look after them, and I'd get even less nursing in an au pair job. I think I will go with Ralph," added Verity, with sudden decision. "It seems too good an opportunity to turn down."

"Because you want a job, or because you like Ralph?" demanded Amanda. "He obviously likes you, but you'd be silly to let that turn your head."

"My head doesn't turn that easily," retorted Verity. "I don't go round expecting good-looking young men like Ralph to be bowled over by me. I'm too plain."

Amanda surveyed her friend dispassionately, neat, slender and light-moving, vivid intelligence in her dark hazel eyes, and every line of her face alive and young. "You're certainly no beauty," she concluded. "But you're attractive enough in your own way. You're far too impulsive, and you've an over-romantic imagination."

"Yes, Auntie," said Verity meekly,

11

her eyes dancing.

"Oh, I know you'll go your own way, whatever I say," sighed Amanda. "I can't help feeling a bit responsible, because you're younger, and I think you'd have been safer staying at home, and marrying your stepbrother, instead of being on the loose, alone, in a strange country."

Verity pulled a face. "It might have been safer, but horribly dull. In fact, quite unthinkable."

As Amanda had predicted, Verity stuck to her decision, and next morning they parted at Dover, promising to write to one another, and to meet again before long. "If you don't find a decent job, come and join me in Oxford, any time," said Amanda. "And be *careful*."

"Was that a warning about me?" asked Ralph. "She seems to feel responsible for you. Is she a relation?"

"No, just a very old family friend. She thought I was silly to come before finishing my training, but she enjoyed having company on the journey."

Ralph talked little as they drove, but when they stopped for lunch, Verity learnt that he was a surveyor, and worked for a firm of estate agents in Bretton. She gathered that he was an only child, as she was herself, and that his mother was a widow, and guessed that he was a rather pampered and cherished son. "Westfield is a big, old house, in lovely country," he told her. "But it is a bit isolated, with very few buses. I suppose that's why it's difficult to get staff. You'd have to find out where you could live, and you might find it rather depressing, working with very old people all the time."

"I've worked in a geriatric ward, and liked it," she told him. "How old is your aunt?"

"She's only seventy, but she's crippled with arthritis. That's why she had to give up her house. She needs help even to dress, and it was impossible to get anyone who would be there all the time. It'll be too late to make enquiries tonight, so I think we'd better find somewhere for you to stay, and then I'll ring up the home in the morning."

"That's very kind, but I don't want to be a nuisance."

"It's no trouble. Besides, Aunt Janet should be grateful to me for adding one to the staff, seeing how often she complains about the service. If she took to you, you might be able to do me a bit of good in return."

Verity thought of Amanda's remark, that Ralph might have his own reasons for suggesting that job, but it seemed a fairly harmless motive. When they reached Bretton, he stopped at a modest-looking hotel, which offered bed and breakfast. They had one single room vacant, so Verity decided to stay. "I'll ring the nursing home tomorrow morning, then let you know what they say," Ralph told her. "What are you likely to be doing?"

"I'd like to have a look round the town."

"Then you could call at my office.

14

It's near the centre. Anyone will tell you how to find it. Come somewhere round twelve." After giving her the address, he said good-bye, and drove away.

It was too late for dinner, but the hotel provided Verity with coffee and sandwiches, and then she decided to go to bed, and read for a while. She woke to a sunny morning, and as soon as she had finished her breakfast, she walked to the town centre, wanting to see as much as she could on this first day in England. She enjoyed everything, the walk, the shops, an ancient castle, her eyes and mind busy with new impressions, finding the country at once strange and new, and yet very familiar to her imagination. She easily found the estate agents office, and Ralph told her that he had arranged to take her to the nursing home that evening.

"Mrs. Hall said she would be glad of extra staff, but seemed rather doubtful about taking someone on for a very short time," he told Verity. "Still, she

15

was interested, so I thought you'd want to go and see her."

Verity thanked him, found a place where she could lunch economically, then went for a bus ride. She liked the countryside of rolling hills and green meadows enough to feel that she would like to stay for some time.

It was dusk when she arrived at Westfield with Ralph, but there was sufficient light for her to see that it was a large, solid, Victorian style house, set in a big garden. Mrs. Hall was younger than she expected, certainly no more than forty. She asked Verity about her nursing experience, and about her trip to England, looked at her references, and then said: "I'd like you to work here, but you would be the most junior member of the nursing staff, and would have to do perhaps more than you'd want of the least popular hours. I mean evenings and week-ends. A lot of the nurses are married, and they do like to have as many evenings and weekends free as possible."

"That wouldn't worry me," Verity assured her. "I don't know anyone here except Ralph, so I'd probably have very little to do at weekends and in the evenings."

"Then you'd be a real asset. My one doubt is about how long you would stay. Elderly people don't like continuous change, and find it very unsettling when someone leaves, just as they've got used to them."

"I can understand that," agreed Verity. "But I'm only staying one year, and I want to see as much of the country as I can, in that time. If I like the job, and you like my work, I wouldn't mind staying until the end of the year."

"January and February are the nastiest months of the year in this country. You wouldn't much enjoy travelling then, so why not stay until the end of February? Or at least until the end of January?"

Verity was reluctant to tie herself down for too long, but she liked Mrs.

Hall, and thought she would be a nice person to work for, and the salary she offered was satisfactory, so she agreed to stay until the end of January, if she could find convenient lodgings, adding: "If the weather's horrible, I could always stay an extra month, if you want me to."

Mrs. Hall gave her two addresses in the village, of people who let holiday flats, and Ralph drove her to the first. Verity's ideas of English villages were on the romantic side, so she was disappointed to find, not a thatched cottage, but an ordinary little terrace house. It belonged to an elderly lady, Mrs. Rudd, who said the flat was vacant, and she would welcome a winter let. It consisted of a bedroom, a bathroom, and a sitting-room with a small kitchen area, and seemed clean and comfortable, if rather dull, so Verity decided to take it, and paid a week's rent in advance.

"I'll help you to move on Saturday," Ralph told her. "You'd better shop in

Bretton, and then I can take that, as well."

"You've been very helpful, and I'm extremely grateful. If I can ever do anything in return, you've only to let me know."

"Well," he glanced at her sideways, "if you feel like that, you could always be extra attentive to Aunt Janet. It couldn't do me any harm."

"Is she rich?" asked Verity, bluntly.

"You think I'm very mercenary? Well, maybe I am," he laughed unoffendedly, "but I'm not the only one. Aunt Janet married a very rich man, much older than herself, and he left her all his money. She has no near relatives. There was a sister, but she married a rascal, and Aunt Janet never forgave her. She and my grandfather were cousins, and the only other relatives are another cousin, still alive, but older than Aunt Janet, and her son and daughter. The son got divorced ten years ago, and Aunt Janet has never forgiven him for that."

19

"She sounds a very unforgiving character," commented Verity.

"You can say that again. Once blot your copy-book, and you're finished, as far as she's concerned. That leaves Aunt Mildred's daughter, and her daughter, Janet, and me. At present, Janet's the favourite. I can't stand her, so naturally I'd rather Aunt Janet left *some* of her money to me. Wouldn't you?"

"I expect so," agreed Verity. "What's your Aunt's name?"

"Marshall. If you don't like the idea, forget it."

"Certainly not. One good turn deserves another. But I would do all I could for your aunt, anyway."

The next day was wet. Verity wrote to her father and Amanda, and then went for a walk in the rain. On Saturday morning, she shopped, and packed her purchases into Ralph's car when he came for her. He helped to carry her things up to the flat, then suggested that as it was a fine afternoon, he should show her a bit more of the countryside. He drove through winding lanes to a small seaside resort. The sea was still a delightful novelty to Verity, and she revelled in the salt air, and the sight of brightly coloured sailing boats. After tea together, Ralph drove her back to her flat, and she spent the evening unpacking, and settling in.

2

VERITY began work next morning. She found it was ten minutes uphill walk from her flat in Melbury Village to the nursing-home. Mrs. Hall took her round the house, introducing her to some of the residents and staff. The place was bigger than she had realised, with a modern addition built on at the back. She did her best to remember the names of residents, and various details about them supplied by Mrs. Hall. Naturally she took particular note of Ralph's Aunt, a severe-looking lady, who had one of the best ground-floor rooms, in the new extension, with windows opening on to a paved terrace and garden. A few old people were confined to bed, some chair-bound, but most of them seemed able to get around. Mrs. Hall told her that they nursed sick people there, whenever possible, sending only the acutely ill to hospital, but Verity did not think she would be doing much real nursing, as most of the nursing staff were better qualified than herself.

The work was very different from that in a big hospital, but by the end of the day, Verity felt that she would like it well enough to stay for the promised four months. As they were getting ready to leave, the senior nurse, Mrs. Grey, told her: "I think you'll do very well here. Most of the residents seem to like you, and you're a very good listener."

"I suppose that's as good a way of wasting time as any," commented Olga, the nurse next youngest to Verity.

"I don't consider it a waste of time," returned Mrs. Grey. "You can work and listen at the same time, and the residents like to feel that we're interested in them as people, that they're not just a job."

"I enjoy listening," said Verity. "Some of the people here have had interesting lives, and still have very lively minds."

"Then go on listening, and making them feel that you are interested," advised Mrs. Grey. "But don't get too involved with any of them, and don't have favourites. The other residents soon notice, and don't like it. And don't fall in love with Dr. Webber."

Verity spluttered with laughter at this unexpected ending. "Who's Dr. Webber? And why the warning?"

"One of a group practice in Bretton. We see more of him than of any other doctors, and he's a very high-powered charmer indeed. He has most of the old ladies eating out of his hand, and too many young ones, at times, so be warned!"

"He's on the make," said Olga. "He always sets out to charm the old people who have the most money, Mrs. Marshall and Colonel Nesbit. And he's as vain as any peacock."

"Oh, well, we all meet professional charmers in hospital," said Verity.

"They don't charm me, but thanks for the warning."

She walked back to her flat, enjoying the cool evening air, and reflecting on the day. She liked all the staff at Westfield except Olga, and that was a pity, because they were nearest in age. She was a pretty girl, but very bossy. She shared a flat with Ruth Manson, who was a little older, and might be quite nice, but she seemed to follow and copy Olga in everything. Verity reached her flat, and looked around with satisfaction. It was very modest, and a bit cramped, but it gave her a fine free feeling of independence, for the first time in her life, and she was very glad that she had chanced to meet Ralph in Paris.

She had her first real encounter with Ralph's aunt next morning. She carried breakfast trays to several different rooms, including that of Mrs. Marshall, and afterwards helped her to bath and dress. She found her quite agreeable but a little intimidating. "I believe you are a friend of my nephew," she said, giving Verity a long, appraising look. "He says you met in Paris."

She made it sound as though there must be something immoral about meeting anyone in Paris, Verity thought.

"We met on a sight-seeing tour. I was with another Australian girl, and Ralph was alone, and we made friends," she explained.

"And so he arranged this job for you."

"He knew that I wanted to get a job as soon as possible, and suggested that I might get one here. It suited me, because I particularly wanted to see the West Country," she added, wondering if Mrs. Marshall suspected that Ralph had an interested motive for the suggestion.

"How old are you?" asked Mrs. Marshall, rather abruptly.

"Twenty."

"And what do your parents think of your coming so far alone? Or have you relations in this country?"

"Not that I know of. My mother's dead, and my father wasn't keen on my coming, but he didn't try to stop me."

"Have you any brothers or sisters?"

"No; only a couple of step-brothers."

Mrs. Marshall's catechism stopped there, to Verity's relief. She wanted to make a good impression, for Ralph's sake, but felt that Mrs. Marshall strongly disapproved of young girls travelling the world alone, and probably disapproved of her on that account alone.

Some time later, she carried lunch to one of the most disabled residents, Colonel Nesbit. He was blind, and partly paralysed, after a stroke, so she had to stay, and help him with his meal. "You don't sound English," he remarked. "Where do you come from?"

"Australia. I'm afraid it's not most people's favourite accent."

"But it's the voice that matters, and you have a lovely voice, warm and young, and lively. Tell me what you look like."

Verity laughed. "That's impossible. I don't know how other people see me. "But because she liked him, she did her best. "I'm just twenty, middling height and rather middling colouring, neither very fair nor very dark, and rather on the plain side."

"And modest, that's obvious," he commented, in amused tones, "What colour eyes?"

"They're a bit of a mixture, not quite grey or green or brown, but a bit of each."

"Hazel, my favourite colour. My wife had hazel eyes."

Verity glanced at the bedside table, then realised that a photograph would be useless to a blind man.

"Tell me what you're doing here, while I eat," he went on. "Have you friends or relations in this country?"

Verity told him about her sudden decision to accompany Amanda, though not the reason, then went on to tell him about the journey, but had only got as far as Rome when he finished his lunch. "You must tell me the rest another time," he told her. "I shall look forward to it. I shall ask Mrs. Hall to let you bring my meals as often as possible. You don't *fuss*, as Olga does, and you enjoy everything so thoroughly it's a pleasure to listen."

Verity was delighted with this praise, and decided to spin her account out as long as possible, as he seemed to enjoy it. Shortly afterwards, she saw Dr. Webber for the first time, but he was passing along a corridor with Mrs. Hall, and she received only a quick impression of a tall man who walked with a light tread, dark, with strongly marked features.

"I've just seen Mrs. Grey's high-powered charmer, and I was rather disappointed," she remarked light-heartedly to Olga. "I imagined he was better-looking."

"He's nothing special, but he thinks he's everyone's pin-up," answered Olga, so sourly that Verity wondered if Dr. Webber had shown a disappointing lack

29

of appreciation of her pretty face.

She took Colonel Nesbit's tea, and brought her story as far as Paris. When she spoke of Ralph, she learnt that he knew Mrs. Marshall well. "We were near neighbours for many years," he told her, "an admirable woman, and generous, but very proud. She probably hates to feel dependent on others now, however willingly help is given."

Verity considered this remark thoughtfully, wondering if that could be the reason for the slight chilliness of Mrs. Marshall's manner, and not suspicion of Ralph's motives. She looked at Colonel Nesbit's fine, expressive face, and thought that he must find it very difficult to accept his much greater disabilities, but there was no chilliness or resentment in his manner.

She enjoyed her work even more as the residents gradually became individuals to her, people whose likes, dislikes, and peculiarities she was beginning to know; some cheerful, some rather complaining, some talkative, some reserved. She saw a good deal of Mrs. Marshall, and felt that she was more friendly than at first, but she was one of the reserved ones, and Verity suspected that she did resent her dependence on others. Mrs. Salter and Mrs. Cuthbert were two very different types, and much easier to please. Mrs. Salter was eighty, and sometimes rather muddled, but always cheerful and talkative, and very appreciative of Verity's gifts as a listener. Mrs. Cuthbert was about the same age, and equally talkative, with a passion for gossip. Her day was made, if she was first with some small item of news about any of the other residents, or the staff, and she seemed to be incurably inquisitive about other people's incomes. At least it kept her from being bored! thought Verity.

Although she had been warned against having favourites, Verity could not help liking Colonel Nesbit more than any of the other residents. As he was confined to his own room, it could annoy no one. She saw a good deal of him, and always took in his meals, while she was on duty. Olga had usually done this before her arrival, and she seemed to resent being superseded.

"You have a real nose for money," she once commented spitefully. "You always pay most attention to the richest people, Colonel Nesbit and Mrs. Marshall. Just like Mrs. Hall. Have you ever wondered how she managed to buy a place like this, at her age?"

"No, I can't say that I have."

"She was a nurse in an old people's home, the same as us. A rich old lady with no relations took a fancy to her, and left her all her money. She put it into this place, and runs it in partnership with her husband. And they make a very nice profit on it."

Verity considered this information with interest. "Well, I think she made good use of the money. It's very comfortable, and most of the residents are happy here. But it's rather silly to accuse me of trying to do the same, when I shall only be here for a few months. And Mrs. Marshall has quite a few relations."

"But she doesn't much like any of them. And Colonel Nesbit has no near relatives."

As Verity got on with her work, she reflected that Olga was probably accusing her of her own motives. She had sometimes wondered why she had chosen to work at Westfield. It was less lively than a big hospital, and she had no real liking for the elderly residents. But now a number of small things added up, the unkind remarks about her having a nose for money, the tale about Mrs. Hall, and the valuable ring she had once shown Verity, telling her that it had been a gift from a resident who had died a few months earlier. She could not help concluding that Olga thought that attentions to old and often lonely people could produce profit over and above her salary, and that was why she resented Verity's being given her previous job of taking

Colonel Nesbit's meals to him. And she wondered if Colonel Nesbit had sensed this, and that was why he did not like Olga.

Verity was supposed to have two days off each week, but two of the staff were on holiday, so she had agreed to have only one off during her first week, on the Friday. She was quite glad of the extra money, to save towards seeing more of the country, later on. Ralph rang her up on Thursday, to ask if she would have tea with his mother next day, and spend the evening with them. Verity would much rather have done some exploring of the surrounding country, and she wondered if Mrs. Blake wanted to inspect her, to see if she were a suitable friend for her son, but she was too grateful to Ralph to think of refusing.

As it was a wet day, she consoled herself with the thought that it would not have been very pleasant for walking, and got the afternoon bus to Bretton. She spent some time shopping, then found her way to the small suburban house where Ralph lived with his mother. Mrs. Blake, a smartly dressed woman of about fifty, gave her a cordial welcome, and her eyes ran over her with interest. Although strangers, they found plenty to talk about; Paris, Verity's impressions of England, and her work.

"When I went to see Aunt Janet a couple of days ago, she said you were the best young nurse they'd had for some time," Mrs. Blake told her. Verity was very surprised by such a favourable opinion from Mrs. Marshall, and wondered if it were the reason for this friendliness, if Mrs. Blake thought that she could help her son's cause. "Have you seen her great-niece, Janet?" she went on.

"No, I don't think so."

"A thoroughly spoilt girl, and not even pretty. I can't believe that Aunt Janet really likes her better than Ralph; but she likes to play one relation off against the others, favouring

35

first one, then another."

"She probably likes to feel that she still possesses some sort of power," suggested Verity, but she was rather embarrassed by these family confidences, and wondered if Mrs. Blake misunderstood her friendship with Ralph. But for his suggestion of a job, they would have parted at Dover, with no more regrets on his side, she was sure, than on hers.

It was rather a relief when he came in from work. His easy friendliness made dinner into a pleasant meal, and not too long afterwards, he packed her shopping into his car, and drove her back to Melbury. "Perhaps we could have an evening out sometime," he suggested. "When will you be off?"

"I don't know. I may have different hours next week, and I won't know until tomorrow."

"Oh, well, I'll probably see you sometime when I come to see Aunt Janet."

Saturday afternoon was fine and

sunny enough for many of the residents to sit outdoors. During the afternoon, Mrs. Grey asked Verity to persuade Mrs. Salter to come in from the garden. "She has no visitors of her own, and she keeps on joining groups of people who have, and monopolising the conversation," she told her. "One of them has complained, so see what you can do. I don't want her upset, and she likes you."

Verity soon found Mrs. Salter, talking nineteen to the dozen, and obviously enjoying herself more than the unfortunate resident whose visitors had been taken over. When Verity approached her, she said, in tones of kindly reproof: "It's rude to interrupt other people's conversation."

Keeping a straight face with difficulty, Verity said: "But you promised to show me the photographs of your grandchildren this afternoon, and I was looking forward to seeing them."

She had already seen them twice, but was sure Mrs. Salter would not remember, and she found this bait irresistible. Verity steered her indoors, helped to find the photographs, and then admired them for the third time. She knew that Mrs. Salter's son was dead, and that her daughter in Canada, and her children, were her only near relations.

They were just reaching the end of the collection, when the door opened, and Dr. Webber came in. He glanced from one to the other. "Mrs. Hall said something about trouble, but everything seems all right."

Mrs. Salter hailed this possibility of a fresh audience with delight. "Oh, don't go, Doctor. Come and look at these photographs of my grandchildren, and my greatgrandson. I've been showing them to Verity."

He shut the door, and came over to her, with an expression of amused resignation, and settled down to look at the photographs, and comment on them. Verity lingered, tidying up the things Mrs. Salter had scattered, in her search for the photographs, but held partly by curiosity about Dr. Webber, after the various remarks she had heard about him.

It was the first time she had given the doctor more than a passing glance, and she realised now that he managed to be very good-looking without having any regularity of features. His eyes were dark blue, clever and amused, his hair thick and dark, his hands square and powerful, and his skin was tanned to an agreeable brown. Verity had been fully prepared to dislike Mrs. Grey's high-powered charmer, but found herself liking him instead, because he was willing to waste a fair amount of time in order to please a muddled old lady. He was showing great interest in the photographs, although she suspected that he, too, had seen them several times before.

He put the last photograph down, and looked directly at her. "You're the new Australian girl Colonel Nesbit has talked about. He says he enjoys his meals quite differently, now that he has you to talk to."

Verity flushed with pleasure. "He's got such a lively mind, it's easy to interest him."

"Perhaps so, but time must hang heavily for a man who was used to a very active life, so I'm very glad to know that he's got a fresh interest. It's done him good."

He left, and Verity put the photographs away, and got Mrs. Salter's tea. Then she took Colonel Nesbit's tray, and admired the display of red roses which had appeared in his room. "They're Fragrant Cloud," he told her. "Their scent is so lovely, they're my favourite rose. Randall Webber brought them over, a present from his mother. They've always grown good roses at Easterbrook."

"Does he live somewhere near here?" Verity asked.

"Randall? Oh, he has some kind of flat in Bretton. His parents live at Easterbrook Farm, and used to be near neighbours of mine. There've been Webbers at Easterbrook for a good few generations, and I believe it was a disappointment when Randall didn't want to farm, but there are three boys and the middle one is farming along with his father, now."

Sunday was usually a busy day, and there seemed to be even more visitors than usual. Mrs. Marshall seemed to have most of her family there, Ralph and his mother, and three people Verity had not seen before. When she took in tea, Mrs. Marshall introduced her to the three strangers.

"This is Ralph's Australian friend, Verity Lawson — my cousins Mr. and Mrs. Raymond, and their daughter, Janet. Verity's the same age as you, Janet, and seems to be doing very well in her profession. It's a pity that you can't find something equally useful to do."

Verity found herself the target of three pairs of resentful eyes. Flushed with embarrassment, she escaped as rapidly as she could. She could not even feel flattered by Mrs. Marshall's praise, because she felt that she was only being used to play off one relative against another, and she resented it. Ralph came out into the corridor after her, and asked if she could come out with him on Friday evening. Verity considered his friendly face. "I hope you're not being influenced by that favourable remark of your aunt's," she said finally.

He laughed with genuine amusement. "I know her much too well, and I did ask you the other day. We could get a meal, then go on to a disco, or cinema, or a drive, whichever you'd like."

"I'd enjoy a drive, but you must let me pay my share."

"We'll see. I'll come for you between six and seven."

Sometime later, Verity went back to remove the tea tray, and stayed to do one or two things for Mrs. Marshall. Her visitors had all gone. Feeling a little natural curiosity, she asked: "What does your niece do?"

"She's at art school. Learning pottery," answered Mrs. Marshall, in a tone of the utmost contempt.

"But that's very popular these days. I like to draw and paint myself."

"But you don't expect to earn a living by it."

"No, I'm not nearly good enough."

"And neither is Janet," retorted Mrs. Marshall. Then a few minutes later, she added: "Vultures!" When Verity gave her a very startled glance, she enlarged: "My relations, all of them. They sit around me, eyeing one another, and wondering who will get the best pickings."

"Really!" commented Verity gravely. "Then it's to be hoped they have plenty of patience, because they'll probably have a long wait."

Mrs. Marshall looked grimly amused. "And at the end of it, they may find that I've left most of it to charity." Verity wondered if this was a hint to her, that she could not count on Ralph's expectations, but she felt unexpectedly sorry for Mrs. Marshall.

Many old people might envy her comfort and security, but Verity didn't think she found it adequate compensation for her loss of independence, and she seemed convinced that her relatives cared only for her money. Perhaps she repelled affection by such suspicions, but it was not a happy situation.

3

IN her second week at Westfield, Verity had Monday and Friday as her days off. Monday was a bright, breezy day, so she packed a picnic lunch, and set off to explore the hills behind the village. She found a lane beside the church, which twisted and turned uphill, passing a couple of houses and a farm, then turned into a rough track, which led up to a wide expanse of sheep-nibbled turf. She paused to get her breath, and to admire the soft green charm of the country, then followed a green track across the top of the hill.

She found a good place to eat her lunch, and lingered for some time, enjoying the sunshine, and a breeze that smelt of warm earth, heather and gorse. Then she walked on along the hill, until she came to a place where the path dipped steeply downhill. The smooth green slope was irresistible, and she ran down it like a whirl-wind, only to brake sharply near the bottom, when she saw that a man was watching her, a little way down the side of the hill. He climbed up to her path, and as he drew near she recognised Dr. Webber. He looked at the wind-whipped colour in her cheeks, and the sparkle in her eyes, and said: "You've certainly got a fine turn of speed. Have you been in this country long?"

"No, only two weeks, and this is my first opportunity to see the country near Melbury. It's beautiful."

"I think so, but being a native, I'm prejudiced. I'm free this afternoon, so would you like me to take you to look at a few local beauty spots? My car's just down the hill."

Verity hesitated. She didn't want to seem rude, but she had been thoroughly enjoying her solitary walk, and she still felt a lingering prejudice against him. Noting the hesitation, he looked amused once more.

"If you'd rather go on walking, just say so, it's a lovely day for it. But you'd get more photographs with that camera if you came."

This suggestion tipped the scales for Verity. If it was a good day for walking, it was an excellent day for photographs, and she had not yet taken many. "I'd love to go, as long as it doesn't upset your own plans."

"I had none that won't keep," he assured her. "Most people are at work on Monday afternoon."

And that, reflected Verity with rueful amusement, probably explained why he was willing to waste the afternoon with her. They went down the side path to his car, parked in a narrow lane. "Are there any places you'd particularly like to see?" he asked.

"No; everywhere's new to me, and I'm afraid I don't know very much about the country just here,"

"Then we'd better start with Selworthy. Everyone goes there."

He drove through a maze of lanes and byways down to the main coastal road, then, some miles farther on, took another lane to Selworthy. The thatched cottages surrounding the green, the little stream, and the beautiful old church matched Verity's mental picture of England better than anything she had yet seen. She took several photographs, and then Dr. Webber took two of her with the village in the background, for her to send home. Afterwards, he took her to see several almost equally lovely villages in the Vale of Porlock, and she finished her films. Then he turned his car along the coast road.

"I'm expected at home for tea, so will you come with me?" he asked her.

"If you're sure they won't mind having a complete stranger."

"Quite the contrary. My mother was a nurse, and she'll want to ask you all about Australian hospitals."

Several miles later, he turned off the coast road up a steep winding lane, then stopped in front of a solid, grey stone house. Verity looked with interest at the plain, old-fashioned house, set in green fields, and backed by sheltering hills. "Turn round and look at the view," he ordered. She obeyed, and gave an exclamation of delight at the view of sunlit sea, and the distant coastline of Wales.

They went round to the side of the house, to a door which led into the kitchen, and Dr. Webber introduced her to his mother, who was busy getting tea. He showed Verity where she could wash, and afterwards she went into the sitting-room, a big room littered with books and newspapers, also a large dog and a small boy lying on the floor together. The dog was a golden Labrador, the boy a ten-year-old called Nigel, who looked very like his older brother, except that he was shy. Verity could not imagine Dr. Webber being shy at any age or in any circumstances. She looked around the room, contrasting its homeliness with the careful neatness of Mrs. Blake's, and liking it better. This room looked colourful, lived-in, and old, which was perhaps its greatest charm to Verity, coming from a country with a much shorter history.

The middle son and Mr. Webber came in together soon afterwards, and they all sat down to a substantial tea. Mrs. Webber did most of the talking, asking Verity about her nursing training in Australia, then about her work at Westfield.

"Don't you find it rather depressing being with elderly people all the time?" she asked.

"Not so far", said Verity. "I'd rather do less dancing attendance on people, and more real nursing, but then it's fine that most of the residents are well, and still able to enjoy life. And even those that aren't — well, I'd never find Colonel Nesbit depressing."

"No, but he's rather an exceptional person," Mrs. Webber observed. "He's an old friend of ours, and was always very active, even after he retired, so he must find total inactivity very difficult. He doesn't even have any family to help. His wife died twelve years ago, and their only son was killed in Korea. But I've never heard him complain."

"Nor me," agreed Verity. "Perhaps it's partly that he's so interested in things outside himself. And then, though he never speaks about it, he has a very strong religious faith."

"How do you know what he never talks about?" demanded Randall.

"I've sometimes read to him. His choice tells me a good deal."

After tea, Nigel, beginning to lose some of his shyness, took her to look around the farm, which looked well-tended and flourishing, with sleek cattle grazing in the fields. Verity wished that she had kept one or two films. When they left, Mrs. Webber gave her a warm invitation to come again, any time. Randall asked where she was staying, and when Verity told him, said: "Oh, I know that house well. Mrs. Rudd is on

51

our list. I expect she's glad to have let her flat for the winter, for the extra money and the company."

"The money maybe, but I'm not sure about the company. She's always pleasant, but we never talk about anything except the weather, and how awful the bus service is."

He laughed. "Give her time, and she'll thaw. Country people are often slow to make friends."

After he left her at her flat, Verity decided to walk up to the nursing-home, and spend half an hour with Colonel Nesbit, guessing that the evening hours could seem very long to a man who was blind, and did not have many visitors. He greeted her with surprise and pleasure, and then asked what she had been doing with her day off. After talking about some of the places she had seen, she read to him for some time.

"There's not a big variety of books in the library here," she remarked, after she had finished. "What happened to your own books? I'm sure you must have had plenty."

"I told John Graham to take any that he wanted, and then give the remainder away."

"Mr. Graham comes to see you quite often, so why not ask him to bring some of your books, anything you particularly like," Verity suggested, "and I could read them to you?"

"You might not like my choice equally well. And anyway, a girl of your age shouldn't be spending any of your free time here. You should be out seeing the country, and making new friends."

"I thought *we* were friends!"

"I like to think so. All right then," he agreed, "I'll ask John to bring a few books, but will you enjoy reading history, biography, or poetry?"

"I expect so, though it might depend partly on the poet."

"What about Browning?"

"He's not exactly my favourite poet," Verity admitted. "But I don't know his work well."

"You often remind me of one poem by him, about a man who complained that his wife was too easily made glad. That man must have been a terrible kill-joy. Easily made glad, it's a lovely quality; don't lose it."

Verity walked back through the quiet of the country night, thinking of that last remark. It was the nicest compliment that she had ever been paid, and this had been her most enjoyable day, since she arrived in England.

The next day, she and Olga were preparing to give one of the very oldest residents a bath. They passed Dr. Webber in the corridor.

"Will you find it difficult to get those films developed?" he asked, as he stopped to speak to her. "I could have taken them, if I'd thought."

"One of the nurses has promised to take them," she told him, "and I'll collect them next time I'm in Bretton."

"Well, let me see them some time."

He passed on, and as the two girls

went into the old lady's room, Olga asked inquisitively: "What was that about? What films?"

"I happened to meet him yesterday afternoon," said Verity briefly, "and he took me to Selworthy, and one or two other places, and I took some photographs."

"Oh! Well, don't let it give you ideas," said Olga, rather nastily. "I've been here longer than you, and I know that Randall Webber likes new faces, and variety. He asked me out several times when I was first here, but I soon found out that he'd taken up with several others when they first came, then dropped them just as quickly."

"I have no ideas of any sort," returned Verity, very shortly. She did not like Olga, and she very much disliked the way she gossiped across their elderly patient, as though she were an inanimate object, without ears, or feelings. Verity had already decided that Olga did not like old people, and that she did just what she had accused her of doing; fussed around those who had most to give. Lonely old ladies appreciated extra attention from someone young and pretty like Olga, and they often gave her presents. Verity had become quite a favourite with many of the residents, partly because her Australian background made her something of a novelty, but also because she had unusual gifts as a listener. Lately, Olga had become thoroughly spiteful, and Verity suspected that she regarded her as a rival for favours from her old ladies.

On Friday morning, she went shopping in Bretton, and collected her photographs. After lunch, she climbed the hill behind the village, and sat down in the sunshine to have a second look at her photographs. The sound of hooves made her look up, and she saw a solitary rider coming at a fast gallop along the green trackway. She sat watching, then suddenly realised that it was Dr. Webber again. A minute later, he saw her, pulled up the horse, dismounted, and came across to her. "Are those your photographs? Any good?" he asked.

He dropped on to the ground beside her, and Verity handed over her photographs. He looked at them with interest. "They're good, all of them. I like this one I took of you. Will you send that one home?"

"I expect so. It's just a pity they cost so much," she lamented. "I want photographs of all the places I like, but at the same time I want to save all I can, so that I can see as much of the country as possible. I'm only here for a year, and I can't expect to be paid a lot, when I'm only half-trained."

"Wouldn't it have been more satisfactory to have finished your training before you came here?"

"Oh, yes; and that's what I intended to do, only I wanted to get away from a very unwanted suitor."

"He must have been a *very* importunate young man, if you felt you had to put half the world between you!"

Amusement gleamed in his eyes, and Verity wished she'd held her tongue, guessing that he thought her attractions were not of the sort to inspire strong feelings. "He wasn't," she answered lightly, "but he happened to be my step-brother, and that created a very unfortunate domestic situation."

"It sounds rather an immoral proposition, to marry a stepbrother, doesn't it?"

Verity laughed. "Yes, it does but for no reason. His mother married my father when I was ten, and I liked him very well as a brother. But to marry him would be deadly dull. I couldn't even think of it. Unfortunately, he took the huff, so did his mother, and that made life very uncomfortable for my father, so I decided to remove myself. I thought of New Zealand, but an old friend of mine was coming to England, so I decided to join her. I've loved it."

"I hope you continue to enjoy it." He got to his feet as he spoke. "We're one short in the practice, so I've only got a couple of hours off, and it's time I was going. Do you ride?"

"No. This looks a lovely place for it, but I'm sure it would be too expensive."

"We've several horses, and I'd teach you, if you wanted to learn, only I never have enough time. One of our group has retired, and we've not yet filled the vacancy. When I've only a couple of hours, like now, I find riding the best way to get plenty of fresh air and exercise in a short time."

He swung himself into the saddle in one easy movement, waved to her, and started back along the track. Verity watched until he was out of sight, with a touch of envy. It was a beautiful horse, but probably no more enjoyable than walking. She told herself. She put her photographs away, walked a little farther, then stretched out to enjoy the sunshine, until it was time to get ready for her date with Ralph.

He agreed to let her pay for her meal, but not to share the cost of the petrol.

They chose a fairly modest-looking place, and over dinner Verity told him about the different places she had seen since they were last together.

"I know Randall Webber, but not well," said Ralph. "We don't go to that group, but I've seen him around at parties, usually accompanied by some very glamorous bird, and a good variety of them, so — "

Verity frowned, though not at the warning implied in the broken-off phrase. She felt that she had been warned quite often enough already. Two modern expressions which grated on her were "bird" and "dishy". She felt that they dehumanised people, but if she voiced her objection to her contemporaries she was usually laughed at, or called a prig, so she kept silent, thinking that Colonel Nesbit would agree with her. Ralph broke into her thoughts, asking: "Now you've seen my cousin and rival, what do you think of her?"

"I've seen her, but that's all," Verity

protested. But then she added: "If I were in your aunt's shoes, I'd rather leave my property to you."

"Unfortunately, Aunt Janet has a rather low opinion of men. I'd be quite happy with a share, but she says she intends to leave everything to one, because the Chancellor will get the lion's share, anyway."

"H'm," said Verity thoughtfully. "That may be true or not. I think she likes playing power politics with money, just to keep everyone guessing. Praising me on Sunday was only done to annoy Janet and her parents."

"Partly, but I think she does have a very good opinion of you, now that she knows you better."

Verity glanced at him uneasily. She didn't want Ralph to think friendship with her would help his cause. "She might leave everything to charity. Or she may not have made a will."

"Well, in that case I would get a half share. But I don't think either's likely. Aunt Janet's far too managing not to make a will."

"I think it's sometimes just the very managing people who put off making a will, because they can't bear to envisage a time when they won't be there to go on managing. Anyway, apart from her arthritis, your aunt's a tough, healthy woman, who may well reach her hundredth birthday!"

"You're probably right, so it's just as well I don't count on anything." Ralph laughed, and Verity's heart warmed to him. She had been thinking that he thought a bit too much about his aunt's money, but now she felt that, if Mrs. Marshall left him nothing, he would be disappointed, but then laugh it off in the same light-hearted fashion.

After dinner, he drove to a smallish, seaside resort, and they walked the length of the prom together. When he stopped at her flat, Ralph kissed her goodbye, with more enthusiasm than Verity wanted. She returned his kiss, because she liked him and enjoyed being friends, but she did not want to become emotionally involved during her short stay here, and she had a nagging doubt that at least some of his enthusiasm might be due to Mrs. Marshall's praise.

"We must have another evening out, before long," he told her.

"I enjoyed it very much, but I'm working different hours next week, mid-day until late evening, and I've promised to work next Friday, so that someone else can go to a party."

"Well, we can fix something later," he answered, so easily that Verity felt reassured.

Next day, the weather turned cooler and soaking wet. On Sunday, Mrs. Marshall's relations were all visiting her again. When Verity took in tea, she spoke to her in a much warmer manner than usual, and she felt very conscious of unfriendly eyes watching her suspiciously. She sympathised with Mrs. Marshall, up to a point, but she did dislike being dragged into family rivalries.

The new shift she was working was unpopular with other nurses, but Verity liked having mornings free, and did not mind working late, now that the days were growing shorter. Most of the staff looked after a certain number of residents, in one part of the nursing-home, so that they could get to know them, and their individual likes and dislikes. Verity had been switched around to a variety of jobs at first, but now found herself working mainly among a group of residents in the new part of the house. They included Mrs. Marshall, Mrs. Salter and Colonel Nesbit, but Verity thought looking after him was more pleasure than work.

When she brought him his tea one day, she asked: "Would you mind if I drew a sketch of you some time? I can draw and talk at the same time."

"I didn't know you were an artist," he said in surprise.

"That's much too grand a name for it," Verity insisted. "I draw and paint a little for my own amusement, and I've

64

often thought I'd like to make a sketch of you."

"But you could have done it any time, without asking, and I'd have been none the wiser."

"That would be an unforgiveable liberty!" exclaimed Verity, in shocked tones.

He laughed, and patted her hand. "I wouldn't have minded, but, no you *never* would think of doing it. Whoever chose your name chose well. You know what it means? — True, genuine. It suits you perfectly."

"You do pay the nicest compliments!" she exclaimed. "But I was given it as a family name. It was my grandmother's second name, and I believe her mother's too. Then you wouldn't mind my making a sketch?"

"Not in the least. I'm only sorry that I won't be able to see it."

Verity worked on the drawing, at intervals, whenever she had a little time, leaving her sketch book in Colonel Nesbit's room. She was putting the finishing touches to it on Friday afternoon, when Mrs. Hall and Dr. Webber came in. She got to her feet, hurriedly gathering her materials together, but Dr. Webber caught a glimpse of the sketch, and unceremoniously took the book from her. "That's an excellent likeness," he remarked. "Don't you agree, Mrs. Hall?"

"Remarkably good. I'm sorry you can't see it yourself, Colonel. You'd like it."

"I've been doing a little at a time, when I had to be here," Verity told her.

"You don't need to excuse yourself to me," Mrs. Hall laughed. "You're one of the nurses I'd never suspect of slacking on the job."

Verity tucked the book under her arm, picked up the tea-tray, and departed, still a little embarrassed. Making that sketch, and feeling pleased with it, were among the few bright spots of that week. The weather had been bad, and an epidemic of autumn colds was sweeping through Westfield.

The miseries of coughs and snuffles had made many of the residents cross and difficult to please. She had had only one day off, and then it had poured all day.

Being off on Sunday morning, she went to church for the first time since she had come there. Several of the local people spoke to her in a very friendly way, and Mrs. Rudd walked home with her. Verity felt that she was beginning to be accepted as part of the community, even if only a temporary part.

4

SEVERAL of the nursing staff were down with colds, as well as the residents, so Verity had agreed to work on Monday, from nine to five-thirty. She did not really mind, because the weather was still very wet, and it meant a little extra money towards seeing the country, when spring came. It was raining hard when she left the nursing-home that evening. She paused to put on her waterproof hood, and Dr. Webber came running down the steps just behind her.

"I'm going through the village, so I'll give you a lift," he said. "You might as well get home dry." He got in beside her, and asked: "And what do you think of our climate, now?"

"It's very much as I expected," she said, smiling.

"It's certainly in one of its worst

moods. How do you come to be working on Monday? I thought you were always off, then."

"There are several nurses off with colds, so I agreed to work today," Verity explained. "I couldn't do much in this weather."

"Perhaps not, but I'd never recommend non-stop work in your job. You need reasonable breaks."

"You seem to be working yourself," Verity commented dryly. "Have you changed your day off?"

He grinned broadly, and stopped at her flat. "There's not a hope of a whole day off while we're still short-handed, and all these colds and things around." He turned to look at her, as she was about to get out. "I've had an idea. I've finished for today, so why don't we cheer each other up? Don't go in and cook something on your gas ring, come out to dinner with me instead, then we could dance, or something afterwards. It's just what we both need."

Verity looked back at him, too

startled for any ready reply.

"How long will it take you to get ready?" he asked.

"Ten minutes."

"Do you expect me to believe that?" He laughed. "I'll give you quarter of an hour, twenty minutes at the outside. I'll come in and talk to Mrs. Rudd."

"Well, don't talk about cooking on gas rings, or she might feel insulted. I have a nice little electric cooker in my flat."

She ran upstairs. She had travelled light, so there was no temptation to waste time choosing what to wear. She got into her prettiest dress, a silky one, patterned in soft blues and greens, and did her hair and face as swiftly and neatly as she did most things with her hands, then found suitable shoes, bag, gloves, and coat. She paused for a swift glance at herself in the mirror, slim and young and flushed with excitement, dark eyes glowing, then ran downstairs with a light step and a light heart.

Dr. Webber looked at his watch.

"Only just over ten minutes! I wouldn't have believed it."

He drove on to Bretton, telling her that he would have to look in at the surgery, but would not be long. It was in a big Victorian house on the northern outskirts of the town, and he soon re-joined her. "Anywhere particular you'd like to go?"

"No; it's all new to me here. I'd enjoy anywhere, it's so unexpected," she said lightly.

"Fine! I know one hotel where they have dancing on Mondays, even out of season."

As he drove out on to the road, Verity had a vivid picture of him, having a gay social life, sampling the attractions of various luxury hotels, always in the company of a succession of glamorous girls, and she didn't bother to ask herself how a busy general practitioner could find either the time or the money for it. Perhaps that was because it seemed so far removed from her own life, but it wasn't an evening for practical thoughts. He drove fast and well, through the thickening dusk, and came to a large coastal resort. They drove along the brightly lit promenade, and stopped outside a large hotel. Inside, Verity was met by flower-scented warmth, and an air of luxury. She glanced around with bright, observant eyes, but looked very young and subdued. Then she sensed amusement in her companion's eyes, and her face broke into a sudden smile.

"I've never been anywhere quite so luxurious as this," she told him frankly. "Isn't it very expensive?"

"Wickedly expensive, but I thought a little extravagance was just what we needed, at the end of a trying day. Let's just enjoy it, and forget Westfield. And away from there, the name is Randall," he told her. "Tell me, didn't your unwanted suitor ever take you for an extravagant night out?"

Verity grinned, catching his infectiously light-hearted mood. "You're forgetting that we'd grown up more or less as brother and sister. He'd have thought it a frivolous and wicked waste of good money."

"Then you were quite right to turn him down. Though, he might have been saving up for a mortgage!"

"Even before he'd asked me!" Verity's eyes danced. "You could be right, though. He was far more astonished than hurt by my refusal, and I'm sure he thought I was very frivolous and imprudent, to turn down such a good, safe offer."

"I doubt if prudence is your strong suit," he said shrewdly.

"Not yet, though I may come round to it in time. I've had rather too much of it all my life. My mother's father had a roving disposition, never stayed long in one place or one job. My mother hated their restless life, so she wanted security and all the solid virtues. She got them, when she married my father, and so did I! So, you see, I don't want to settle down without having been anywhere, seen anything, or had any small spice of adventure."

"You won't find much adventure in an old people's home."

"I'm only there for four months, and many of the old people have had very adventurous lives. They enjoy talking about them, and I like to listen. It was such a different world, when they were young."

They had a leisurely and luxurious meal, and lingered over it enjoyably. Randall was a good talker, but a good listener too, with a quick mind and a lively sense of humour, and Verity was in a mood to enjoy anything, to laugh at anything. It was partly the sheer unexpectedness, and partly that she had been missing the companionship of people of her own age. Ralph was her only friend there, and the Westfield staff were mostly a good deal older. Randal was friendly, natural, and very easy to talk to, and they drifted happily from one subject to another, not knowing, or caring, how they got there.

Later on, they danced together, and

Verity became aware of several interested glances in their direction. She had too realistic an estimate of her own looks to suppose they were directed at her, but she enjoyed the novelty of having an escort who was likely to take people's eyes wherever he went. She was a good dancer, with a natural grace and gaiety of movement, and neither of them was in a hurry to leave. When they did, they found that a full moon was competing with the fairy lights on the prom. They walked across the road, and stood watching the moon making a path of silver across the dark sea, both suddenly silent and very reluctant to move, until Verity shivered in the chilly night air. Then they turned back to the car.

When they stopped at her flat, Verity said thank you for the evening. "I enjoyed your company," Randall told her. "It was exactly the prescription we both needed. Even the weather seems to have improved."

Verity said good-night, and went softly upstairs. When she switched on her light, the familiar dullness of her flat brought her abruptly down to earth, with a painful bump. Out of all the happiness and gaiety of the evening, one hard fact emerged, she had fallen in love with Randall Webber as swiftly and as thoroughly as she did most things. She had been warned against that very thing, apparently to no avail, and she knew that she was foolish, but she could not regret that it had happened.

She woke next morning with a feeling of the morning after the night before. Last night, she had still been a little intoxicated. The evening and Randall's company had gone to her head like wine, and she had found it shattering, and yet wonderful to be fathoms deep in love. Today, she was cold sober, and everything looked very different. She had started by being prejudiced against Randall, but he had charmed her against her own will, and apparently without effort on his part. His charm, she felt, was not of the outside only, but sprang from a generous nature and an infectious, out-going vitality. But how many girls had felt the same as she did about him?

Yesterday evening had been no more than a wonderful accident, she told herself firmly, a chance meeting at the end of a dreary day, a sudden impulse on Randall's part, and that was all. If she expected anything more, then she would be disappointed. He had not even ended the evening with a kiss, though, on the whole, she was glad he had not. It would have meant too much to her, and not enough to him.

Getting up, she looked at herself in the mirror, a small-boned face with clear, pale skin, straight, lightbrown hair, a short, tilted nose and a wide mouth, thoughtful eyes of dark hazel. "You're certainly no beauty," Amanda had said, "but you're attractive enough in your own way," and Verity thought that summed her up quite accurately;

attractive enough to be a pleasant companion for one evening, but not a girl whom men would readily fall in love with. Her stepbrother was the only one who had shown any inclination to do that, and Verity did not believe he was really in love with her. He just liked the safe, the known, and the familiar. But Randall was too attractive not to have had plenty of other girls in love with him. She supposed they had got over it, and married someone else, but she simply could not convince herself that she would do the same. He seemed everything her heart desired, possessing humour, vitality, and intelligence, yet with a curiously sober mind for such a lively personality, as she had discovered, last night. She wondered if that stemmed from his stable, traditional farming background; for her that sober gentleness of mind provided the final touch which made him irresistible. She felt that he liked her, but then he seemed to like most people, and she would be a fool if she allowed herself to hope for anything more from him.

Two air-mail letters, arriving by the morning post, did something to cheer her up, but news from home seemed to have become strangely remote, compared with these new and bewildering feelings. She was not quite sure whether she wished she had stayed at home, safely and unadventurously, though never that she had married Ian. She found things to do during the morning, and had succeeded in scolding herself into a more cheerful frame of mind by the time she left for work. She was not going to inflict her problems or miseries on the old people at Westfield. Besides, some of them, like Colonel Nesbit, showed an uncomplaining courage which made her troubles seem trivial.

She saw no more of Randall that week. There were still some people ill, with colds or worse, but his visits seemed to be made in the morning, before she came on duty. Ralph rang up, to suggest another evening out together, and as she was off on Friday, she accepted. She was rather put out when he took her to the same resort as Randall, but all resemblance ended there. They ate in a smaller, cheaper place, and followed it by a film Ralph wanted to see. Verity found him pleasant company, and felt reasonably sure that he liked her in a similar, easy, comfortable way.

On Sunday evening, she took in Colonel Nesbit's supper tray, and was startled to see Randall sitting with him. He got up, to make room for the tray. "This is a purely social visit," he explained. "I was called in to see someone else, and dropped in here for a brief gossip. I'm going now. Will you be off tomorrow?"

"Oh, yes; we have a full staff again."

"Well, I'm off in the afternoon, and I wondered if you'd like to see a bit more of the country?"

"I'd love to," she told him, her face radiant with sudden happiness.

"Where are you thinking of going?"

asked Colonel Nesbit. "Where would you recommend?"

"If it's wet or dull, Wells. But if it's fine enough, Dunkery Beacon. I know Verity would like either."

"A good choice, we'll go to one or the other, and I'll come as soon after two as I can. The afternoons are getting shorter now."

As the door shut behind him, Colonel Nesbit said: "I do hope it's fine enough for the Beacon. You could go to Wells any time, but you should see the view from Dunkery before winter begins." He could not have sounded more pleased, Verity thought, if he had been going, miraculously, to see that view again, himself. Unconsciously, her hand gave his shoulder a little affectionate squeeze, and he smiled at her, with that quickness of perception she had learnt to know. "I shall look forward to hearing about it afterwards. And we all enjoy showing strangers the places we love most."

And that, thought Verity, combined

with the fact that not many people were off on a Monday, was probably why Randall had asked her. She continued to remind herself of this, at frequent intervals, but it did nothing to diminish her happiness. Too easily made glad, Colonel Nesbit had said, and he was about right, she decided.

She woke to a bright morning, and the sun was still shining when Randall came. He looked at the gay expectancy in her eyes, and smiled.

"It's a perfect day for Dunkery," he said. "You'll have to walk the last part, but I don't suppose you'll mind that?"

"Oh, no. It's not a day for sitting still."

He took the coast road, then turned inland, up a road that climbed steeply through tawny October woods, then came out on to open moorland, still climbing. At the highest point, they got out of the car, and paused to admire the view of moors, woods and fields, clothed in a riot of autumn gold and crimson, a shining blue streak of sea just visible beyond the coastal hills. Then they turned along a rough, stony path to the Beacon. Up there, on the summit of the hill, they had an even wider view, including the distant hills of Dartmoor. The brisk breeze whipped Verity's hair about her cheeks, as she took several photographs, and Randall told her the names of some of the hills. Then they walked a little way down the hill, and found a sunny, sheltered place to sit.

Verity spread out the map she had recently bought, and Randall leaned companionably over it, pointing out various places they could see. She looked around her at the cloud-shadows racing across the sunlit moor, at his hand on the map, large, brown, and powerful, felt the warm friendliness of his shoulder against hers, and happiness bubbled up in her heart. They sat talking in easy snatches, about anything or nothing, until Randall decided that they would go down to Porlock for tea. They wandered around the village afterwards, then drove down to the Weir, and by the time they left there Verity had finished another lot of films.

"Do you only draw people, or places as well?" asked Randall.

"Oh, places are easier than people, and sketches are cheaper than photographs. Unfortunately my family prefer photographs," she said ruefully.

"How like a family! I thought that sketch of Colonel Nesbit was excellent. I'd like to see some of your others."

Verity flushed with pleasure. "I wished I'd had my sketch book with me, to do one of your farmhouse," she said, then flushed again, wondering if that sounded too much like a hint for a second invitation.

"Well, perhaps you'll have it with you some other time," he said easily. "You're never off at week-ends are you?"

"No, because everyone else wants to be off then, and it doesn't matter to me. But I will be off next week-end.

I've got Saturday, Sunday and Monday together, so that I can go and see my friend in Oxford."

"Then I hope the weather keeps fine. You'll find plenty to see there."

"So Amanda says. But if it does keep fine, I may come back on Monday morning." Again, Verity half-regretted the words as soon as they were spoken, wondering if Randall thought she would be returning early in the hope of seeing him. Rather hastily, she added: "Amanda has to be back at work then." But in her heart, she doubted if that was her reason.

Randall made no comment. Coming to the turning for Melbury, he drove past it, and on to West Quantoxshead. Verity had not been there before, and they got out of the car to watch the sun going down behind the western hills, in a blaze of splendour, before going back to Melbury. "It was a lovely afternoon," she told him.

"I certainly enjoyed it." Randall smiled slowly, lifted his hand, and drew one finger down her cheek in a curiously gentle and affectionate gesture. Then, rather abruptly, he got out and went round to her door. "I hope Oxford comes up to your expectations."

Verity went up to her flat in a mood of wondering uncertainty, asking herself all sorts of questions to which she could find no satisfactory answers. Had Randall known that, this time, unlike the other evening, she had wanted him to kiss her? Did he prefer to keep things on a purely friendly basis, because he was determined not to get involved with any of the Westfield staff? And did he realise that she was in love with him? And that she would rather spend half an hour with him than have an extra day in Oxford? Although she could find no answers, the happiness of the long afternoon lingered in her heart. This time it had not been due to a fortunate accident, so she could feel that Randall must enjoy her company, even if not quite as she enjoyed his, and there had been something very personal in that small farewell gesture, which made it seem, perhaps, more meant than a routine, good-bye kiss.

5

RANDALL had taken Verity's films to Bretton, so she collected them on Saturday, on her way to the station. She inspected them on the train, found them very satisfactory, then carefully put those in which he figured into a different envelope. She had no intention of letting Amanda see those, and then listening to her comments, questions and advice. She reckoned that she had quite enough sense for most things. Where Randall was concerned, she had been swept off her feet by a tide too powerful to be resisted, but she still retained enough commonsense to know that she would be foolish to hope for anything more than liking and friendship from him. She didn't need Amanda to point that out.

She thoroughly enjoyed her week-end.

The weather was fine. Amanda took her sight-seeing in the daytime, and in the evenings they talked, comparing experiences and impressions since they had parted at Dover, looking at each other's photographs, and some of Verity's sketches. By a happy coincidence, the train time-tables fitted in with Verity's plans. The best and quickest train was early in the morning, so she could tell Amanda that she would rather get that, and then do some shopping before getting the bus to Melbury. She knew that she would have stayed until Tuesday morning, but for the fact that Randall often had some free time on Mondays. She had no reason to expect to see him, but, if she stayed in Oxford, she would be wondering all the time, if she were missing the chance of an hour or two with him. That was how foolish she had become.

She got a quick lunch when she reached home, then climbed the hill, and walked along the summit to one of the highest points. There, she sat down, and got out her sketch-book. From that vantage-point, she had a fine, wide view of the country. More important she had a clear view of anyone coming up one of the side paths. Randall might be working, she told herself, or have better things to do than climbing a hill to meet her, but her attention was very divided as she began to sketch. Her interest gradually increased, and she jumped when a shadow fell across the page. She looked up, her face lighting into vivid life, and Randall sat down beside her.

"And how did you like Oxford?" he asked.

"Very much," she answered. "But I thought I'd rather be back here today. It's easier on the feet."

"That sounds like a surfeit of sight-seeing!"

"Amanda had Saturday and Sunday off, and she was determined to cram all she could into the time, but we both enjoyed it."

He glanced down at her unfinished

sketch. "That's not bad, but I liked the one of Colonel Nesbit better. Did you do any sketching in Oxford?"

"No time. Amanda wouldn't stay in one place long enough, so I just took photographs."

Randall glanced through her sketch book, very much enjoying a spirited likeness of Mrs. Salter. Then he asked: "Do you want to finish your sketch, or shall we walk to the end?"

"The sketch doesn't matter. I was only filling in time," she answered, and then thought she seemed to be continually saying things that might be better left unsaid. But she was too glad that he had come to worry about that.

He suited his stride to her step, and when they reached the end of the path, said: "I'm going to the farm for tea. Will you come with me? You'd be very welcome."

Verity accepted, but when they arrived at Easterbrook there was another visitor there, a fair-haired girl who greeted Randall as an old friend.

"Father sent me to see if I could borrow something from your father," she told him. She cast a swift, inspecting glance over his companion, which made Verity wonder if the borrowing was only an excuse, and then took confident possession of Randall. Verity went to sit by Nigel, who was still rather shy and silent, but growing more friendly.

Janet was still there at tea-time, and Randall had to be back for evening surgery. He and Verity left immediately after tea. It was almost six when they reached Melbury; so he stopped only just long enough to let her get out, then shot off again. She went up to her flat, happy and unhappy, both at the same time. She had got her wish, to see Randall again, but he had probably climbed the hill for air and exercise, rather than to meet her. She wondered if he found her as obvious as she had found Janet. But Janet was a much prettier girl than she was.

She unpacked her week-end case,

then spent the rest of the evening drawing Randall from memory, not for the first time. Some of the sketches pleased her, some did not, and were torn up, but none of them satisfied her completely. Those that she did keep were quite separate from her other sketches. They were too revealing for her to risk anyone else seeing them.

It was pleasant, when she returned to work, to be told that she had been missed.

"That was the best meal for days, with you to season it," Colonel Nesbit told her. "I expect Olga means well, but she's very dull."

"Like the stepbrother who wanted to marry me," Verity laughed. "He was *very* well-meaning, but deadly dull. My father thought I shouldn't have turned him down, and gloomily predicted that I'd probably end up married to an amusing wastrel."

"I think you were quite right. Dullness is in the grain, and can't be cured, and a lively mind and a dull one would never be happy together."

Verity always enjoyed the time she spent with Colonel Nesbit, talking while she attended to his needs. On her present shift, she usually had time to read to him, during quiet spells in the evening. He introduced her to writers that were new to her, and they both enjoyed exchanging opinions about the writers, and their views.

On Friday morning, she went shopping in Bretton in the pouring rain, and just missed the only morning bus back to Melbury. She arrived at the stop just in time to see it vanishing up the road, and stood there considering what to do. The next one would not be until afternoon. Even if she filled in time in the town, she would be late for work. Much though she liked walking, she did not relish the thought of walking six or seven miles in pouring rain, carrying a heavy bag of shopping, and she might still be late. A taxi was the most convenient solution, but she grudged the extravagance. She decided to get a bus that would take her slightly over half the distance, and which was nearly due, and walk the remainder.

When she got off the bus, it was still raining hard, and blowing half a gale. About half a mile along the road, she reached a small village, and the sight of a parked car brought her to a startled halt. It was a very ordinary car, well splashed with mud, but she thought she would have recognised it, even without the number plate. A quick, familiar step made her turn, suddenly covered in confusion at being found gazing like that at his car.

"Don't tell me you go walking in this for pleasure!" exclaimed Randall, as his eyes ran over her dripping figure.

"Certainly not! Especially not with a load of shopping. I missed my bus," Verity explained, "and got one that took me part of the way, and then I thought I recognised your car."

"There are hundreds of that make and colour, though perhaps not all as dirty."

Verity sensed amusement in the words, and the colour crept up her cheeks again. He opened the passenger door with one hand, and took her bag in the other. "Get in," he said kindly, "and I'll save you the rest of the walk."

"I don't want to take you out of your way," she protested.

"I've got to go to Westfield sometime." He put her bag in the back, and walked round to the other door, then looked at her thoughtfully. "I've got a better idea. I'm doing a round of country visits and intended to go in somewhere for lunch, so will you join me?"

"All dripping wet like this?"

"I'm not bone-dry myself. If you'd rather go straight back, and get dried, I'll take you. But I'd enjoy your company."

Verity was surprised by the warmth in his eyes. The dull day suddenly became bright, and her dark eyes glowed. "I'd love that, but I'm working today, because of having Sunday off, and I'm on duty at one."

He glanced at his watch, "I'll get you there by then, and there's time for me to make a couple more calls before lunch."

While he was in the first house, Verity looked at herself in the driving mirror. With damp hair plastered to her cheeks, she looked even less of a beauty than usual, but a little flush of pleasure glowed in her cheeks, and her eyes were filled with bright happiness. She decided that she would pass.

When Randall returned from his second call, he drove to a smallish country hotel. Verity removed her wet mac, wishing she was wearing something smart underneath, but she looked very neat and slender in pants and a dark green pullover. "I'm afraid you won't have much choice," Randall told her, "but the food is always good here."

"I'd only have had time to boil an egg, if I'd walked the rest of the way", she returned, not caring what she ate. She looked at him across the table, at his lively, generous face, the warmth of his quick smile matching the humour in his eyes, and she felt a singing happiness that had no real reason or justification.

Their talk wandered casually from one thing to another, Randall telling her various things about the country, including odd items about his unknown past, to which she listened with fascinated interest.

It was still raining hard when they left the hotel, and Randall suggested driving her straight to Westfield. "Oh, no, I'll have to put my shopping away, and get into uniform!" she exclaimed, quite glad of this reason. Either Randall was unaware of gossiping tongues and inquisitive eyes, or so used to them that he didn't care, but she did.

For once, she arrived at Westfield a little late. As she started on her first job of the day, Olga, also just starting, asked: "And what had you been doing with Randall Webber?" In response to Verity's startled glance, she explained:

"I passed as you were getting out of his car, but you were too engrossed with *him* to notice me."

Verity certainly had not noticed Olga's car. She would happen to pass just then! she thought. Aloud, she said: "I don't have my own transport, like you. I missed my bus, and was lucky enough to get a lift. That's all."

"Well, just wait until someone newer and prettier turns up, then see how quickly Randall drops you," Olga predicted spitefully.

Verity moved away, not bothering to answer. As she had never imagined that Randall was in love with her, she could not be disappointed if that did happen, she told herself. She tried to be content with the knowledge that he liked her. Sometimes she was, but not always.

On Sunday, all of Mrs. Marshall's relations were visiting her and when Verity went into the room, she felt a wave of silent hostility directed towards her, and suspected that Mrs. Marshall had been using her friendship with

Ralph to annoy the other half of her family. She disliked the feeling of being used by warring family factions, so when Ralph came out to ask her to go to a party with him, she was glad to have the excuse that she would be on night duty. He looked genuinely disappointed, but then added: "Well, you'll be free on Saturday afternoon, won't you? I've nothing fixed for then, so would you like to see Wells or Glastonbury?"

Verity looked at his friendly face, decided that he was much the nicest member of his family, and said: "I'd love to see Wells."

Next morning, she noticed that her landlady was coughing continually. They had become much more friendly, so she went down and asked if she could do anything to help. "Oh, it's only a nasty tickle. I've had a cold for the last few days," Mrs. Rudd told her.

"I may be wrong, but it sounds like bronchitis to me. Have you had it before?" Mrs. Rudd admitted that she had, but resisted Verity's suggestion that she should get the doctor. "Well, at least go to bed now, and let me get you some breakfast," said Verity. "No, I don't know where you keep things, but I've got plenty of food. I'll fix a tray, and bring it down."

Mrs. Rudd allowed herself to be persuaded, and afterwards she agreed to let Verity ring up the surgery. As a secretary answered the telephone, Verity did not know which doctor would come, but thought it would probably be Randall. She did several things to help Mrs. Rudd, then went upstairs to her own flat. When she saw Randall's car stop at the gate, she ran down to let him in, took him in to Mrs. Rudd, then went back upstairs. A little later, there were feet on the stairs, and he appeared in the open doorway. "So this is where you live! It looks very comfortable, if a little dull."

"The view of the village street is seldom dull," she countered.

He came into the room, and sat

down. "You were quite right to send for me," he told her. "I've left Mrs. Rudd some tablets, and told her to stay in bed and keep warm. Someone will have to shop for her, and get her meals. I might be able to get a home help, but — " He glanced at Verity, half-smiling.

"Well, of course I'll get her anything she needs. She's used to me by now, and I'm sure she'd rather have me than a complete stranger. I'm on night duty for the next two weeks, so I can easily fit it in."

"I thought you'd say that," he smiled. "I'll come in again on Wednesday, in the afternoon, so that you can get a decent sleep in the morning."

Verity found it easy to look after Mrs. Rudd, and she had several offers of help from neighbours, most not needed, but she was glad to accept a lift to the shops. On Wednesday, Randall said that Mrs. Rudd should stay in bed until he came on Friday or Saturday, so Verity told him that she would be out on Saturday afternoon. She more than half-wished that she had not agreed to go with Ralph, although at the same time she felt that it was a matter of indifference to Randall who she went out with.

On Friday, he allowed Mrs. Rudd to get up, but advised her to stay indoors and in the warmth for a few more days. Verity arranged with a neighbour to get her tea on Saturday, and she would be back to get her evening meal.

It was a dull afternoon, but the sun came out for a while, just as they reached Wells, and Verity was able to take several photographs. They spent a good while looking around the cathedral, and the little town, then had tea, and Verity amused herself by making another quick sketch of Ralph. "It's good. I might show it to Aunt Janet; ask her if she'd like to keep it," he said.

"I wouldn't risk it. She might consider it pure conceit on your part, perhaps on mine, too, as I did the drawing."

"But it's good. And she likes you."

"I'm not sure," said Verity slowly. "Sometimes I think so, sometimes not. On the whole, I don't think she very much likes anyone on whom she depends for help. If she does praise me, it's to keep your cousins guessing."

"You may be right," he agreed with amusement. "Perhaps I'll just keep it myself, to be on the safe side."

When on night duty, Verity was in charge on the ground floor, with a senior nurse upstairs, where there were more bedrooms. She usually started by taking round bedtime drinks, and helping some of the disabled into bed. Once everyone was settled for the night, she sometimes had very little to do before morning, but that Saturday she soon realised that it was not going to be a peaceful night. Not long after everyone was in bed, she was alerted by a succession of muffled thuds and thumps. She traced them to Mrs. Salter's room, and found her sitting on a chair beside an open drawer, wearing only a nightdress, and surrounded by what appeared to be most of the contents of the drawer. She beamed at Verity, and asked: "Are you going to help me to pack?"

"To pack what?" asked Verity, looking for her dressing-gown, and putting it round her.

"Don't you know that I'm going home tomorrow?"

"But it's nearly midnight. You'll need a good sleep, so come back to bed, and I'll see to your packing tomorrow," Verity told her. She knew that Mrs. Salter no longer had any home except Westfield, but thought she would have forgotten all about this notion tomorrow. Always a little muddled, she seemed to have become much more confused. She persuaded her back into bed, bundled the scattered garments back into drawers, to be tidied next morning, then got her a cup of tea. She stayed with her while she drank it, and when she put out the light Mrs. Salter already looked half asleep.

Silence reigned for over an hour, then she answered a call from one very disabled resident. As she was helping the old lady back to bed, another bell rang, and continued to ring as though the owner was keeping a finger on the bell. Verity hurried to answer it, as soon as she was free, saw that it was from Mrs. Marshall's room, and found her sitting up in bed, looking extremely angry, while Mrs. Salter, in her night-dress, sat on the bottom of the bed talking happily.

"I've been awake for hours, and had only just got to sleep, when I was woken by Mrs. Salter," Mrs. Marshall told her, in outraged tones. "If you can't prevent this sort of disturbance, you're not fit to be left in charge."

"I only came to say good-bye," Mrs. Salter explained, in eminently reasonable tones. "I'm going home this morning."

"But it's still the middle of the night, so come back to bed." Again Verity persuaded Mrs. Salter back to bed,

106

praying that she would remain there this time. Then she went back to Mrs. Marshall. "I'm very sorry you were disturbed," she said. "Mrs. Salter is even more muddled than usual tonight."

"I'm not blaming her, poor thing. It's your job to prevent such disturbances. And need you have taken quite so long to answer my bell?" Mrs. Marshall snapped.

"I was in Miss Robson's room, and had to see her back into bed," Verity explained patiently. "She can't walk alone. Can I get you a hot drink, or a sleeping tablet?"

"No; I want nothing except peace and quiet. And that isn't much to ask."

Verity withdrew, thinking that if Ralph had overheard that exchange he might be a lot less certain that his aunt liked her. Of course, Mrs. Marshall was angry, but Verity suspected that her real feelings showed more plainly when, for once, she lost control. She went back to Mrs. Salter's room. She was still in bed, looking almost asleep, so she left her. Everything remained peaceful, but she took the precaution of looking into the room twice, and each time Mrs. Salter seemed fast asleep. She began to relax, though still keeping a watch on that door. Some time later, she heard sounds of movement, again from Mrs. Salter's room. When she opened the door, the light was on once more, drawers open, and clothes scattered around. Mrs. Salter turned, took a step to meet her, and tripped over a large travel bag, falling with a crash that seemed to shake the whole house.

Verity dived for the emergency bell, then returned to her. The old lady was shaken and rather dazed by the fall, but said she was not hurt. Verity put the eider-down over her, a pillow under her head, and then the senior nurse arrived, and decided to waken Mrs. Hall. She joined them very quickly, but by that time a number of other bedroom bells were ringing, so Mrs. Hall sent Verity to attend to them. She went round telling rudely awakened residents what had happened, and got hot drinks for some of them, to help them back to sleep. When she went back to Mrs. Salter's room, Mrs. Hall told Verity that she was not going to risk moving Mrs. Salter until a doctor had seen her, and that Randall was already on his way. "I'll go and get dressed," she added, "then I'll go with her, if she has to go into hospital. You pack a few things in a bag, just in case."

Mrs. Salter seemed reasonably comfortable on the floor, and remarkably cheerful, partly because she seemed convinced that Verity was packing for her to go home. Verity was still looking for necessary items among her scattered possessions when Mrs. Hall came in again with Randall. After examining her, he decided that Mrs. Salter would have to go into hospital for an X-ray. He went to the telephone, and Mrs. Hall decided to make a quick cup of coffee for them both. Verity stayed with Mrs. Salter, finishing the packing, then tidying the room, and worrying that she might have been to blame in some way for the accident.

When the ambulance men arrived, Mrs. Salter suddenly seemed to realise that she was being taken away from all these familiar people and things. Her cheerfulness abruptly vanished. Mrs. Hall assured her that she would come with her, but Mrs. Salter turned away from her, and grabbed Verity's hand. "No, you come," she insisted.

They exchanged a glance, and then Mrs. Hall nodded. "She's more used to you. Get your coat and go with her. Get a taxi back, and I'll pay."

It was between six and seven o'clock when Verity returned to Westfield. "Have you had anything to eat since you came on duty?" asked Mrs. Hall. Verity had not. "Then go and get something now, even if it's only coffee and biscuits."

Verity got herself a cup of instant coffee, and drank it while telling Mrs. Hall everything that had happened during the night. "Perhaps I should have stayed with her," and she concluded. "But I did glance into her room twice, and she seemed sound asleep."

"You've absolutely no reason to blame yourself," Mrs. Hall told her firmly. "I'd have done just the same, in your place. When you've worked with old people as long as I have, you'll know that it's quite impossible to prevent an occasional fall. Would you rather go home now, and I'll carry on here?"

"Oh, no; I'll stay until the day staff are here."

She was kept busy for the remainder of the time, getting early morning teas, and answering enquiries about Mrs. Salter. Mrs. Marshall asked no questions, and Verity decided that she must have slept through the second disturbance, and was probably a much better sleeper than she thought.

6

WHEN the day staff came on duty, Verity walked back to her flat, and got breakfast for Mrs. Rudd and herself, then went to bed. She never found it easy to sleep in the daytime, but that morning the events of the night persisted in streaming endlessly through her mind. In spite of Mrs. Hall's reassuring words, she kept on asking herself if she ought, somehow, to have prevented Mrs. Salter's fall.

When she went on duty in the evening, she learnt that Mrs. Salter had a fractured femur, that it had been set, and her condition was satisfactory. Unfortunately, she knew too much about the dangers of this, so she did not find it cheering news. She took round the bedtime drinks, and Colonel Nesbit told her that the residents had made a collection to buy flowers for Mrs. Salter, and wanted her to take them into the hospital.

"That was your idea!" she exclaimed.

"No, we always send flowers or fruit to anyone who has to go into hospital."

"I meant that you had suggested my taking them," she smiled.

"Oh, well, I thought she'd like to see you best. I was told that it was you she wanted to go with her. And if you want more reasons, you have a very acute sense of responsibility, so you're almost certain to start blaming yourself, for something no one could have prevented. I can still remember how I used to react, in my service days, if anything went wrong. You'll feel better after you've seen her."

The following night, when Verity came on duty, Mrs. Hall told her that Mrs. Salter had improved a little, and gave her a note which Dr. Webber had left for her. It was just a folded piece of paper, and obviously not private, so she read it at once. "He says he'll be coming to see my landlady tomorrow afternoon, and could give me a lift to the hospital, to see Mrs. Salter. Would it be all right for me to go in then?" she asked.

Mrs. Hall nodded. "Yes, so he told me. I had thought of going to see her myself, tomorrow, but you go then, and I'll go a day or two later."

It might be no trouble for Randall to give her a lift to Bretton, but it was typical of his thoughtfulness in small things, thought Verity. Anxious not to keep him waiting, she saw that she was ready in plenty of time, and then put on her coat while he was with Mrs. Rudd. He told her that he would not need to come again, and Mrs. Rudd could get back to normal life, but gradually.

"Shopping's the most awkward, so I'll do that for her, for the next week," Verity said. "I have to buy some flowers for Mrs. Salter, from everyone from Westfield. Is there a shop near the hospital?"

Randall told her there was, and

stopped outside it, then turned to look at her. "I suppose you're blaming yourself for Mrs. Salter's fall?"

"A little," she admitted. "I was on duty, and I knew she was restless. If I'd stayed with her, or watched her more — "

He shook his head. "No. Westfield's not like a hospital ward, where you can see almost everyone at a glance. The chief reason why people go there is that they value privacy and a certain amount of independence. They pay quite a high price for it, so you must give it to them, even when it involves a few risks."

"That's true," said Verity thoughtfully. "I hadn't thought of it like that."

"It's the same as with very young children. You must take some precautions, but don't draw the limits too tightly. Children must experiment and learn, and old people must feel that they have freedom of choice. I'd rather break a leg than live permanently in some kind of padded cell, no matter how comfortable. I think you would, too, and Mrs. Salter. She's quite a determined lady."

"You're probably right," Verity agreed, her smile spreading from her lips to her eyes. "Thanks a lot, for the lift, and everything." She got out of the car, feeling happier for the reassurance, and for the fact that he was concerned about her feelings.

She found Mrs. Salter in surprisingly good spirits, and very pleased with her flowers. She looked reasonably well, and Verity thought her cheerful disposition might be the biggest help towards recovery. She was glad to give a good report, when she took the bedtime drinks round that night. She told Colonel Nesbit more details about her visit, then paused in sudden recollection. "But you don't know Mrs. Salter, do you?"

"Only from you. She's not one of the people I used to know, outside."

That small word, outside, struck a chill note in Verity's imagination. It suggested that Westfield was a prison, and reminded her of Randall's remark about a comfortable padded cell. It was completely at variance with Colonel Nesbit's usual lively interest in the world, and that made it even more revealing. She put her hand on his, and he sensed her thought with uncanny accuracy. "Well, of course I'd give a good deal to be active and independent again. Anyone would. But most good things bring drawbacks, and most bad ones have compensations, or so I've found," he said thoughtfully. "If I were not here, I would never have learnt to know you, and that is quite a compensation."

"I wish I could believe that," said Verity. Then knowing that he would not welcome too much sympathy, she added: "You flatter so beautifully, I think you must have had a lot of practice, when you were young!"

"Oh, no, I was much too shy. But you're wrong, flattery is insincere praise. I usually mean what I say."

On Monday morning, Mrs. Rudd

asked Verity to come to the phone. She ran downstairs, heard Randall ask if she were free in the afternoon, and her spirits soared sky high. "I'm not doing night duty now, and I've got the whole day off, and nothing planned," she told him.

"I've only got a few hours off in the afternoon, and I wondered if we could go somewhere together, perhaps a drive, and then a walk? It's a lovely day."

Verity agreed, with enthusiasm, which she made no attempt to disguise, then ran upstairs again, much too happy for safety. She did not even bother to remind herself that his choice was limited, on a Monday afternoon. It was enough that he should seek her company.

It was a lovely day, sunny, yet with a crisp tang of autumn in the air. Randall drove to a part of Exmoor that was new to her. They drove along an open road crossing the wide loneliness of the moor, unfenced and unhedged, with hills on either side, then stopped near a patch of green turf, ringed around by gorse bushes.

"It's such a perfect day, it seemed a shame to spend any of it indoors," said Randall, "so I packed a picnic tea. I don't think you require fancy picnic areas, do you?"

"No, I'd much rather have the ground, and the solitude," Verity added, but only to herself.

Randall got out a picnic basket, which held a flask of tea, fresh rolls, strawberry jam and clotted cream. It was a perfect meal in a perfect spot. Afterwards, Verity lay back on one elbow, watching the golden autumnal countryside surrounding them, feeling no need of words in the sunny contentment of the moment. They seemed to be alone on an island of their own making, shut in by gorse bushes, with only an almost empty road and the hills before them. Randall was equally silent, but there was no constraint in their silence. At length, he said: "If you want a walk, it's time we were moving. I have to be back for evening surgery, unfortunately."

Verity got to her feet, rather reluctantly: "I thought it would be completely winter here by this time of year, yet it's quite warm."

"You can only make one safe prediction about this climate, it's not predictable! Some years it *would* be winter, and it may be in a day or two, so let's enjoy the sunshine while we can." Taking her arm in his, he turned along a green pathway, which took them to a small moorland village, with a small old church. There was just enough light for Verity to chance a couple of photographs. Then Randall looked at his watch, and exclaimed at the time, and they walked back a good deal more quickly than they came.

He drove half-way along the open moor road, then stopped again. "Look behind you," he said. Verity turned, and saw the sunset blazing red and gold across the western hills. Randall put a casual arm round her shoulders, and they watched in silence, held by the beauty of the scene. As the sun vanished behind the darkening hills, Verity sighed and turned. Their eyes met and held for a few seconds, then Randall bent and kissed her, softly and lingeringly. The touch of his lips on hers was the sweetest thing Verity had ever known. He lifted his head and looked at her, a small smile touching his lips, hesitated as though about to say something, but then turned quickly away, and re-started the car.

He drove the rest of the way at a fast pace, and left his engine running when he stopped at her flat. "I'm late, and must get back," he told her, but then softened the words by touching her cheek gently, and adding: "Till the next time."

Verity went up to her flat in a daze of happiness. She tried to tell herself that one kiss meant little these days, but it did depend on the person, and on the kiss. She felt that she knew Randall fairly well by now. He was not a casual person, but sensitive and gentle towards other people, and intelligent enough to realise that she was in love with him. She didn't think he was unkind enough, or vain enough, to encourage her, if he did not care for her a little beyond ordinary friendship. All the same, reason told her that one impulsive kiss could not have been as unique, or as wonderful, to him as to her. Probably it had just been the natural end to a lovely afternoon. Thus far reason, but there had been something in the look in his eyes, the touch of his fingers, that made it very difficult to accept mere reason. She gave up trying to rationalise her feelings, lived on the promise of "till next time", and drew another couple of sketches for her private collection.

She was interrupted by another telephone call. This time it was from Ralph. She had difficulty in switching her thoughts from Randall to Ralph, and when he invited her to go with him to a friend's engagement party, that Friday, she felt an odd reluctance to accept. But he had asked first if she were off on Friday, and she had said yes, so she felt she had to.

On the Friday morning, she went shopping in Bretton. She planned to get lunch there, and go and see Mrs. Salter afterwards, but that left her with a good deal of time on her hands. She spent some of it shop-gazing, and was tempted into the extravagance of buying a new dress for that evening's party. She preferred to keep her clothes to a minimum, so that she could travel light, later on, but she was honest enough to admit that Randall was in her mind when she bought it. He was never far from her thoughts, and Christmas was drawing near, with all the possibilities of that season. She told herself that she could not manage any longer with only one party dress. She found Mrs. Salter looking much better, and fairly content in the hospital, and she enjoyed hearing Verity's small bulletin of gossip and news about Westfield.

When she was ready for the party, Verity decided that the extravagance of the new dress was justified. No dress could transform her into a striking beauty, but the simple line of this one made the most of her light figure, and the soft green and white seemed to emphasise the bright warmth of her hazel eyes. Ralph confirmed this opinion.

"I say, you look great," he exclaimed in startled tones. Perhaps the surprise was not very flattering, but Verity laughed, and set off in a happy mood.

The party was being held in a big country club outside Bretton. It was more dressy than some parties Verity had been to, making her glad that she had bought the new dress. Ralph introduced her to several of his friends, and she danced with two or three of them, but mostly with Ralph. Halfway through the evening, she was jolted by the unexpected sight of Randall, dancing with a pretty, darkhaired girl.

She realised that she had no reason to feel surprised. Living in Bretton, he must have many friends there, and Ralph had said that he had met him occasionally at parties. She had kept Randall and Ralph in such completely separate compartments of her mind that it had never occurred to her that they might both have been invited to this party. She found that she did not like it at all, and wondered if she were just jealous, because the girl he was with was much prettier than herself. Perhaps it was partly that, but she soon realised that it was not quite so simple. Although she had often imagined him leading a gay social life, in reality she always thought of him at Westfield, where they shared similar work; or even better, somewhere in the hills, just the two of them together. Seeing him unexpectedly among a crowd, obviously at ease among people who were strangers to her, was a jolt to which she had to accustom her mind. It made her own friendship with him seem thinner and newer, and perhaps very temporary.

Soon after that, she and Ralph made their way to a very crowded buffet, collected food and drink, and took it to a table, which they shared with another couple, both friends of Ralph's. Ten minutes later, Randall appeared with a different but equally pretty girl. This time he noticed Verity, and paused at their table, to say: "I'm glad to see you here, and I hope you're getting to know a lot more people. Perhaps we could have a dance later."

He exchanged a few more comments, with her and with Ralph, then passed on, but Verity's eyes still followed him unconsciously. It was quite late, and probably the end of a very busy day for him, but she noticed that he still looked fresh and alert, and ready for anything, and seemed to be keeping his partner in a state of continuous entertainment. Though she had often told herself that Randall would never be short of attractive female company, she found that it was a very different thing to see it with her own eyes, and unexpectedly painful. She wished that she had not come to this party, and she was glad when Ralph suggested that they should go and dance again, but they had only been dancing for a few minutes when he asked, somewhat abruptly: "How well do you know Randall Webber?"

Verity looked at him in surprise, and answered as lightly as she could: "He's in and out of Westfield several times a week, as you must know."

"As a doctor, but are the nurses on first name terms with doctors at Westfield?" he persisted.

"No," Verity admitted. "Mrs. Hall likes rather formal etiquette there. But I did tell you that Randall had taken me to see Selworthy, and one or two other places."

Ralph said no more, and Verity was thankful to drop the subject. She hated to have any outsider touch or question her relationship with Randall. It was too private and too sensitive to be exposed to other people's curiosity, and she could not help wondering why Ralph was interested. It could hardly be jealousy, as they were only casual friends.

Some time later, she danced with Randall. "I didn't see you here at the start of the party," she remarked.

"No, I was working rather late, and might have given it a miss, only Nigel's an old friend. It's a good party, too. I hope you've made a few new friends."

"I've met a lot of people, but that isn't quite the same as making friends, is it?"

"Hardly. But some new people become old friends in a very short time." Something in the look he gave her made Verity catch her breath, and feel happier.

They danced together for a little longer. Then she danced with Ralph again, and afterwards he decided that it was time they left. Half-way home, he abruptly returned to the subject of Randall. "You know, he's something of a professional charmer, always a good-looking girl in tow, but never the same one for long, so I hope you don't take his attentions seriously."

"What attentions?" Verity almost snapped. Then she pulled herself together. "Look, Ralph, I'm a stranger here, practically a foreigner. You and Randall have both taken me to see more of your country, and I'm very grateful, but I don't imagine that it's anything more than kindness. I'd be delighted to do the same for either of you, if you ever come to Australia."

"Well, maybe." Unexpectedly, Ralph drew in to the side of the road, and stopped. "The thing is, some girls seem to know everything, but you don't strike me as like that."

He sounded so genuinely concerned that Verity forgot her annoyance. "It's very nice of you to be bothered about me, Ralph, but I really do have the normal amount of good sense, and I don't go round imagining things that don't exist."

"Well," said Ralph, rather doubtfully. Then to her astonishment, he reached out, grabbed her, and kissed her very thoroughly and very possessively. Verity emerged from his embrace feeling extremely ruffled, yet in no mood to object. She liked Ralph, was still grateful to him, and did not want to risk his starting another argument about Randall. She was very relieved when he started his car again, and drove on. When he stopped at her flat a few minutes later, he kissed her good-bye in a much more casual fashion, but she still got out of his car very hastily.

She went upstairs feeling that it had been a very mixed sort of evening. She was uneasy about Ralph, wondering why he had suddenly seemed so possessive, wondering if a pleasant friendship was beginning to turn into something she did not want. What had prompted that unexpected embrace — affection, jealousy, or was it just that Ralph believed she could be useful to him at Westfield, and did not want her to be interested in someone else? Before long, her thoughts were all dragged back to Randall. It was the first time she had not been glad to see him. She was clear-sighted enough to know the reason for that, but if anything, that made it seem worse. When they were out together, she could feel that for a brief time he was all hers, but tonight she had had to share him with a lot of other people who had known him much longer and she had not liked it one bit. She had just told Ralph that she had a normal amount of sense, and didn't imagine things that did not exist, but she was afraid that it was not true. Without realising it she had slipped into a ridiculously possessive feeling about Randall, yet his repeated remarks about hoping that she was making new friends set her wondering if he had only taken pity on her, because she was a stranger and very short of friends.

Her uneasiness about the party, and about Ralph and Randall recurred all through the week-end. She was off on Monday, and it rained all morning. About mid-day it changed, and became bright and windy, so she decided to go up on the hill. Apart from the vague hope of meeting Randall, it was the pleasantest way to spend a sunny afternoon. She walked to the far end of the range, then stood there for a while looking across the fields to the choppy, wind-flecked sea. She turned back, conscious of a flat feeling of disappointment, but half-way along the path she saw a tall figure coming rapidly up the side of the hill. Her spirits shot up, and she went to meet him on feet that wanted to run. His long stride soon brought him to her, and she paused, smiling all over her face in the sunshine. His hands shot out, he drew her close, and gave her a quick, impulsive kiss, then held her a little away, looking down at her. Verity wondered if he saw through her carefully casual air, to all that lay beneath it. "You're lucky to have the whole day off," he told her. "I have to be back for evening surgery."

"You're still short-handed?"

"Yes, but not for very much longer. At last, we have agreed on a new partner."

"When does he start? And is it someone you'll like to work with?"

"She, not he," he corrected. "That's been the main difficulty. Both my partners are older than me, and one of them wanted his niece to fill the vacancy, while the other has an antediluvian prejudice against including a woman in *his* group. I kept out of the argument, and now he has finally withdrawn his objections. As to liking to work with her, she lives in Edinburgh, and I've never even seen her. As I said, I kept out of the argument, but I like her uncle."

Verity suddenly remembered having been told that the newest member of the group usually had to do the country round. "Will she be coming to Westfield instead of you?" she said anxiously.

Randall shrugged his shoulders indifferently. "No details will be settled until after she's started. I'm certainly looking forward to having a bit more time to call my own, particularly with the busiest season of the year getting nearer. I've promised to put in a brief appearance at home. You'll come with me?"

"If you're sure they won't mind."

"Why should they? They're well used to it."

As they walked down the hill, Verity pondered over this remark, wondering whether Randall meant that his family was accustomed to casual visitors, or that they were used to his bringing a variety of different girls home with him. It had begun to rain again, before they reached the farm. Randall took her indoors, but then went out to look for his father, leaving her alone with Nigel. He pushed his books aside, evidently feeling that it was his duty to entertain her, but Verity told him not to interrupt his homework for her. He returned to his books, and she took out a sketch book and began to draw him, as he lay on the rug, in frowning concentration. He did not notice what she was doing, and she became so absorbed that she did not hear Mrs. Webber come in, until she glanced over Verity's shoulder, and exclaimed at the drawing, saying it was exactly Nigel.

He jumped to his feet, and came to look at it. "Gosh! you must have done that quickly," he exclaimed. "And I didn't even know that you were doing it. I wish I could draw, or do something unusual like that. All the same, I think it's more like Randall than me."

Betraying colour rushed over Verity's face. "But you are very like Randall," she told him. "I don't suppose you notice that as much as other people do."

The three men surged in as she spoke, and came to look at the sketch, and make amused comments. Mrs. Webber asked if she could keep it, and added: "Have you ever drawn Randall?"

"I've never had as good an opportunity."

Tea was ready, and they left almost immediately afterwards. Randall drove as though in a hurry, and dropped her at her flat with only a quick good-bye. Verity went upstairs, and added one more sketch to her collection, and wondered if Randall had noticed that she had evaded giving a direct answer to his mother's question. She put her pencil down, and let her thoughts drift pleasurably back over the afternoon. Randall might have climbed the hill for fresh air and exercise, but she thought that he had expected to meet her there. She still felt that it was impossible that anyone quite so attractive could fall in love with someone as ordinary as herself, but she found it even more impossible to think that he would encourage her obvious attachment, if he felt nothing at all for her. Deep inside, she felt that something had begun to grow between them, but that was so wonderful a thought that she hardly dared to dwell on it. Instead, she began to think about her promise to stay at Westfield until the end of January. In late August that had seemed too long a period, but now it was the end of October, and another three months seemed all too short. Mrs. Hall had wanted her to stay for an extra month, so she wondered whether to tell her that she had decided to do so. Once Randall's new partner started work he would have more free time, and he might spend some of it with her.

7

VERITY had a good deal more real nursing to do during the remainder of that week, as several people were ill, one of them seriously. Randall was at Westfield every day, and although all contacts there were on a strictly professional level, Verity sometimes thought that he made excuses, even quite flimsy ones, to see her and exchange a few words. Then she would tell herself that that was sheer imagination and wishful thinking. Sometimes, watching him with a patient, she wished she had the skill to draw him as he looked then, in a moment of intense concentration.

As she walked up the Westfield drive on Sunday, Randall drove down it. He stopped, leaned out of the window, and asked: "Are you off tomorrow? And have you made any plans?"

"Yes, I'm off, but I seldom make plans until I've seen the weather."

"Well, I've got to drive down to South Devon in the afternoon, and I wondered if you'd care to come with me? You've not seen anywhere round there yet, have you?"

"No. I'd love to go."

"Fine, and let's hope the weather stays decent. If it does, bring your camera, and we'll go across Dartmoor. Then we'll have dinner somewhere before coming back. I'll come sometime after half-past one."

He drove away, and Verity continued up the drive, walking on air. Randall obviously had to drive to South Devon, so it was natural that he should like some company, and he didn't have very much choice on a Monday afternoon, she reminded herself, as so often before. In spite of this she continued to live in a secret glow of anticipation. Of course she was pleased at the prospect of seeing more of the country, but any place would be

139

exciting to her in his company.

He arrived a little before two, on a bright, windy afternoon. "I'll be going through Exeter, so I can stop for you to take some photographs," he told her. "Or are you feeling too economical?"

"Not where photographs are concerned. I worked overtime on Friday, because of having so many people ill, so I can spend some of the extra cash on the photographs."

As they drove, Randall told her that he was going to see an elderly lady. She had lived at Westfield for three years, and been his patient during that time, but a year previously, her son's firm had transferred him to Newton Abbot, and she had moved to an old people's home in the south, in order to be near him. "She's not been well for some time," he told her, "and she has the notion that her new doctor doesn't know what's wrong. She's written several times asking me to come and see her, so I got in touch with the doctor, and he doesn't mind my

140

coming. She was inclined to fuss about her health, so there may not be much wrong, but if a visit makes her feel better, it's probably worthwhile."

Soon, all the country they passed through was new to Verity. They stopped for a while in Exeter, and at one or two places crossing Dartmoor, and she took photographs at each stop. "Would you like to go through Widecombe?" Randall asked.

"It's not a real place, is it?" Verity asked in astonishment. "I always thought it was just a song."

"The place is real enough, as you'll soon see," he laughed.

Widecombe was their last stopping-place before they drove to the old people's home. Randall suggested that Verity might like to have tea somewhere, while he made his visit, but she preferred to wait in the garden of the home. She had quite a long wait, but occupied herself by sketching the view out to sea. When Randall joined her, he was apologetic.

"I had to listen to a long account about this nursing-home, then tell Mrs. Bennett all about different people she knew at Westfield," he explained. "I thought of calling you in to give her the information, but I don't know when we'd have got away. We're going to Torquay for dinner now, and there's still time enough to take the longer road, around the coast and marine drive."

It was a lovely drive, with dusk deepening into darkness, and quite dark when they drove down the hill into Torquay, with lights glittering all round the bay. Randall drove to a hotel at the far end of the prom, where he had reserved a table by a window, looking out over the dark sea. The food was excellent, but somewhat wasted on Verity, who was too happy to care much what she ate. They talked, laughed, and fell silent, all equally easily, learning more about each other's unknown past, and Verity thought that there was a natural harmony between them; they were serious about the same things, and found the same things funny.

"What shall we do now?" Randall asked, at the end of the meal. "Go straight back, find somewhere to dance, or go for a walk along the front?"

"Whatever you like."

"No, I asked you first," he insisted.

"Then a walk. It's a lovely evening, and I never get tired of the sea."

There were very few others on the prom. Randall put his arm through Verity's, and his hand closed around hers. They loitered along in a happy quiet, paused for a while to look at the lights reflected in the dark sea, and then turned back. "Would you like to go back the quickest way, or across the moors again?" he asked.

"You'll be doing the driving, so I'll leave that to you. Wouldn't you rather go the shortest way?"

"I'm in no hurry for the day to end."

When the road began to climb uphill again, and she realised that Randall had chosen the longer road over the moor, Verity stopped wondering about that last remark, and gave herself up to the sheer joy of being with him. They reached a high, lonely stretch of road, and he stopped the car, switched off the engine, stretched his arm along the back of the seat behind her, and sat silently looking out at the night. Verity leaned her head against his arm, too content with the sense of wordless accord to want anything more. There was very little passing traffic, and after a while Randall said: "On a night like this I can almost believe Dartmoor is haunted, can't you? But of course, Australia is even older. They say it's the oldest continent, don't they?"

"But its human history doesn't go back very far."

After a while, his arm tightened around her shoulder, drawing her close, and when he lifted her face up to his, she responded to his kiss with a heart overflowing with love. All too soon, he lifted his head, and his eyes rested gravely on her. "I could happily spend the rest of the night here with you," he murmured, "but it must be around midnight, and Mrs. Rudd may think all sorts of things by the time I do get you home. It's time we moved."

He released her so abruptly that Verity felt a momentary chill, but then commonsense told her that he was probably right. Neither of them talked as he drove quickly through the night, When he stopped, he dropped a light kiss on her cheek, and she smiled at him wordlessly, slid out of the car, and crept upstairs as quietly as she could.

The glow and brightness remained in her heart all next day. Then on Wednesday the one seriously ill patient died. Death was not new to Verity, after two years working in a hospital, but this death saddened her more than usual, because she had had time to get to know her and like her, and she was not one of the oldest residents.

That day, November came in with gales and lashing rain, blowing away all the warmth of the Indian summer, and Mrs. Hall told her that she would be doing night duty for the next two weeks. Verity did not really dislike night duty, and knew that she had to take her share, but it meant that she was unlikely to see Randall while she was on duty, and if this stormy weather persisted, she was equally unlikely to meet him on the hill, or anywhere else. The winter weather would probably mean that he would be busier than ever.

"Have you given any thought to staying here until the end of February?" Mrs. Hall added. "I'd be very glad to keep you for the extra month, and by then the weather should have improved. At least, the days will be longer."

Verity looked at the grey November day, and the lashing rain on the window, and told Mrs. Hall that she would like to stay for another month. But she was influenced less by the weather than by the thought that Randall's new partner would be starting work soon, and then he would have more time.

She had Sunday and Monday off together, before starting night duty, and both days were soaking wet. She went to church on Sunday, and talked to some of her neighbours afterwards, and wrote a few letters, but when it was just as wet on Monday, time began to hang rather heavily. She went for a couple of walks in the rain, but had to keep to the roads. She was not yet completely acclimatised to the damp cold of an English winter, and her gas fire seemed cheerless and inadequate, and it was a whole long week since she had seen Randall. As the wind strengthened and seemed to be howling threats of winter days to come, her usually cheerful spirits wilted a little, and she asked herself if she had been imagining something between herself and Randall that did not really exist.

Tuesday was wet again, but she decided that any activity was better than none, and got the morning bus into Bretton. She did some shopping for herself, then bought a big bunch of flowers, and went in to see Mrs. Salter. The warm welcome she received, and Mrs. Salter's cheerfulness made her feel better. She stayed for some time talking to her, retailing all the small snippets of gossip she could think of. She had already told Mrs. Salter that her room was being kept for her, and used in the meantime for a few short-stay people, mostly convalescents just out of hospital, and the old lady wanted to know every detail about each of them. Afterwards, Verity had lunch in Bretton, got the bus back, and had several hours sleep before starting work.

The week seemed to pass much more slowly when she was on night duty. She slept in the mornings, and there did not seem to be enough to do in the afternoon and evening, with the weather continuing wet, the days getting shorter and shorter, and very few buses. There was another wave of colds going round the home, and two people were really ill, so Randall was in frequently, but always in the daytime, and she guessed that the bad weather was making him extra busy everywhere.

She had Sunday and Monday off again. On Sunday it was only showery, so she went for a walk on the hill, and returned with soaked feet, counting the days until the end of the week, when she would have finished her stint of night duty. On Monday — showery again — she went for a walk along the road, thinking that she might climb the hill by the lanes and short side-path which Randall usually took. That way, she might keep her feet a little dryer. She had almost reached Westfield when a child on a bicycle came too fast round a sharp bend, and skidded on the wet road. Child and bicycle went down in a tangle, and Verity ran to help. She lifted the bicycle clear, bent over the small boy, and recognised him.

"Why you're Martin Farley," she exclaimed. "Let me see if you're hurt." Both his knees and one hand were cut and bleeding, and he was obviously badly shaken, struggling bravely against tears, but she did not think he had broken any bones. As she helped him to his feet, she remembered that his mother was in hospital, and his father was probably out at work. "I'll take you to Westfield," she told him. "It's only a few minutes' walk. Do you think you could sit on your bike, and I'll wheel you there?" She lifted him on to the seat. "Shouldn't you be at school?" she asked.

"I've a bad cold."

"And now you've got two cut knees as well!"

As they neared the house, Verity saw Randall's car standing outside. She lifted Martin off the bike, and led him inside, just as Randall and Mrs. Hall came down the stairs. They both came over to see what was wrong, and Randall took charge. "Come along to one of the bathrooms, and I'll soon fix those knees," he told him. "It's a good thing you brought him here," he added, with a quick smiling glance at Verity.

He cleaned up both knees, and removed several bits of grit from one, while Martin held on to Verity's hand. When both knees were bandaged, he frowned over his wrist, now swollen and very tender.

"I think it's only a bad sprain," he murmured, "but it would be safer to have it X-rayed. I have to see a couple of people here, and then I'm going back to Bretton, so I'll take him with me."

"His mother's in the hospital at Bretton," said Verity.

"Yes, I know. They'd better ring up his father from the hospital, and then he can take him home afterwards. Perhaps you'd get him some sort of hot drink, while I'm seeing my other patients; and if you could come with us, I think he'd feel a lot better."

★　★　★

Verity got Martin the drink and some biscuits, then tidied up the bathroom.

"What will they do to me at the hospital?" he asked.

"Take a photograph of your wrist, then they'll probably put some strapping round it, and it will feel a lot more comfortable. Would you like me to stay with you until they've finished?"

"Please."

Randall took Martin into the casualty department himself, then left, saying that he was terribly busy. Martin was sufficiently recovered to take a lively, if slightly nervous interest in the proceedings. Randall's diagnosis of a bad sprain was confirmed, and Mr. Farley joined them just after it had been strapped up. "I'll just nip up and see my wife," he told Verity, "and then I'll drive you both back."

As he drove back to Melbury, he thanked her again for looking after his son. "He's too young to be left on his own all day," he told Verity. "It was all right when he was at school most of the time, but he's been off for several days with a nasty cold and cough. And you had no right to be out at all in this weather, Martin."

"The rain was off, and I had nothing to do," the boy said sulkily.

"And now he's got to stay off for the rest of the week, with all this," continued Mr. Farley. "Some of the neighbours have offered to help, but Martin didn't want that. Though I'm not sure after this — "

"I'm not a baby," protested Martin indignantly.

"I'm working at nights, so I sleep in the morning, and have nothing to do in the afternoons," Verity told him. "Would you object to spending some of the day with me, either in your home, or my flat?"

"I'd like that."

So for the rest of the week Verity had a shorter sleep in the mornings, and a nap in the evenings, and spent most of the intervening time with Martin, partly in his house, partly in her flat. He was an independent, intelligent nine-year-old, and he liked to draw and paint, so

153

they occupied quite a good deal of the time drawing together, and comparing their efforts. Fortunately, it was Martin's left wrist that had been injured. Verity made several lively sketches of him, a couple of which were taken into the hospital to be shown to his mother, and she found that the time passed a lot more pleasantly.

The weather was still in a vile mood, and, after a soaking Monday, Verity was glad to get back to work, at her old time, from mid-day until late evening.

"Although it was nice to see you during the night, I'm glad you're back on this shift again," Colonel Nesbit told her. "Meals were so much duller without you."

"I like it better, too," Verity agreed.

A new patient was arriving that afternoon, to occupy the room which had belonged to Mrs. Grant, who had died two or three weeks previously. Her room had been given to a short stay convalescent, but this newcomer was a long stay resident, coming from a hospital some distance away. She was badly disabled by a stroke, so Verity was sent to do her unpacking, and help her to settle in.

Mrs. Bradshaw was in her late sixties, pleasant, but quiet and reserved, and Verity thought that she was one of the people who found it hard to accept dependence on others. Having an independent nature herself, she always felt warm sympathy, for those who valued independence, yet made no fuss when deprived of it. As she unpacked, she talked about Westfield, the people there, and why she, an Australian girl, happened to be working there. She had a gift for making small, ordinary things, interesting and amusing, and felt quite delighted when she was rewarded by a genuine laugh.

Then Mrs. Hall and Randall came in. His eyes flicked across to her for one second, and then he turned his whole attention to Mrs. Bradshaw. Mrs. Hall told Verity to finish the unpacking, so she put the last few things away, and left. Randall usually had a smile for her, and often a friendly word, so the brevity of that quick glance left her with a faintly chilled feeling. And that was very unreasonable, she told herself. Mrs. Bradshaw was a new patient, someone he had not seen before, so naturally he wanted to know all about her case, as quickly as possible.

Some time later, she took in Mrs. Bradshaw's tea. She could not use her right hand at all, which was probably one reason why she preferred to have her meals in her room, to begin with; and she needed some help, although she could use her left hand to a certain degree. She had little to say; probably, thought Verity, because her speech had been affected, and she was sensitive about it.

She took in Mrs. Bradshaw's evening meal as well, and her son came in to see her, just before it was finished. Verity met him again as he was leaving, and he stopped to talk to her and thank her for looking after his mother so well.

"I think she'll be comfortable here," he said, "but she'd be happier at home with me. The difficulty is that I've no one to look after her. I'm at work all day, and my two children at school, and she couldn't be left alone, could she?"

"No," said Verity, very definitely. "But she may improve a lot, particularly if she has a strong motive for getting well, but you should talk to her doctor about that."

"I suppose so, but he's only seen her once. I'd make any alterations to the house that were needed, if it does become possible."

"Then tell her that. A strong motive can be half the battle."

A couple of days later, Verity was crossing the hall, with a book Mrs. Marshall had sent her to fetch, when Mrs. Hall beckoned her. She was talking to Randall, and when Verity went over, she said: "We're discussing Mrs. Bradshaw, and you've seen more of her than I have, probably more than anyone else here, so your opinion is worth more than mine."

She turned to Randall, and so did Verity. His eyes met hers in a coolly impersonal glance.

"I've been talking to her son," he said. "He would like to have her to live with him. That is impossible at the moment, but I think it might be possible in the future, provided she has the will to make a long and persistent effort. Some people have, some have not. What do you think about Mrs. Bradshaw?"

His voice was without warmth, and Verity felt a creeping sense of unease, but tried to concentrate her mind on the question. "I think she could be very determined about something she really wanted, and I think she badly wants to regain some of her independence."

Randall nodded. "Yes, that's my own feeling, but it will be mostly a job for nurses. To begin with, just encourage her to use her left hand as much as possible, and in as many ways as you can, and she should move around her room, with help, quite frequently. That's about all, until she gets a little more confidence." He gave Verity one or two more detailed instructions, then turned to Mrs. Hall. "We'll get a visiting physiotherapist later, but I don't think just yet."

Verity felt herself dismissed. She gave him one quick glance, her eyes young, baffled and hurt, then turned away.

"You've been a very long time," Mrs. Marshall exclaimed sharply, when she gave her the book. "I told you *exactly* where it was."

"Mrs. Hall stopped me, when I was bringing it," Verity explained.

As she turned to leave, two of the residents stopped her, and she had to listen to a long rambling tale from one, and then fetch something for the other. She escaped from the sitting-room at last, but it was very difficult to get even a few minutes privacy at Westfield. In search of it, she went out of a back door to a small covered verandah where the residents sometimes sat in good weather. It was pouring today, and the weather matched Verity's feelings. She leaned against the damp rail, going over in her mind that short encounter in the hall, feeling baffled and sick at heart. Randall had never before spoken to her in that cool, impersonal fashion. The presence of Mrs. Hall never made him less friendly, and she linked it with his ignoring of her on Tuesday. She had felt a vague uneasiness then, and dismissed it as sheer imagination, but today she could not. Something was wrong, but what? He had spoken to her with the necessary civility, and nothing more. They might never have been friends. What had she done?

Then she reminded herself that she had no time for brooding while she was on duty, and went back indoors. She took Mrs. Bradshaw's tea, then Colonel Nesbit's, and for the rest of her time there she tried hard to concentrate all her thoughts on work.

The day seemed much longer than usual, and when it ended at last, she walked back through the wet, blowy night, switched on her gas fire, and sat for a long time beside it, in the dark, tired and bewildered by her thoughts. Something had gone wrong, but what? Olga had repeatedly told her that Randall made a practice of taking up with fresh girls, paying them attentions, then dropping them when the novelty wore off. She had never believed that, and she did not now. It was out of character. The Randall she knew would never be so heartless and frivolous. Then what was it? Had she perhaps read too much into his kindness, and had he just become aware of it, and felt that she ought to realise her mistake? Her mind went back to the night he had stopped on Dartmoor. She had felt closer to him than she had ever felt to anyone before, and had probably shown quite clearly that she was deeply in love with him.

For a few minutes Verity thought

that this must be the answer, until she remembered that she had seen him a week later, when Martin Farley fell off his bike. He had been entirely his usual friendly self then, so that was no solution. She found no reasonable answer to all her self-questioning. Every time she shut her eyes she could see his face, glancing at her with a heart-chilling politeness, and she went to bed a prey to acute misery beyond her worst imagining.

For several days she saw nothing of Randall. His visits were always in the morning, and she wondered if that were coincidence, or if he preferred not to see her. She tried to concentrate her whole attention on her work, and went about it quickly and quietly, but without heart. She spent a good deal of time with Mrs. Bradshaw, with Mrs. Hall's approval, encouraging her to move about, and trying to build up her confidence in ultimate, even if only partial recovery. She got on well with her, but Mrs. Bradshaw seemed unconvinced that she would ever be able to leave the home. On Tuesday afternoon, Verity was helping her to make a slow circuit of the room when Randall and Mrs. Hall came in. He asked Mrs. Bradshaw to continue walking, and stood watching her. He had not even glanced at Verity, but she was acutely and painfully aware of his eyes on the two of them, as they finished their slow perambulation. She could not, and would not, try to hurry Mrs. Bradshaw, but it was a great relief when she got her back to her chair. She turned to go at once, and heard Randall say: "I hope you're doing that quite often."

"Oh, yes, but I don't think I'm walking any better. Do you, Verity?"

Verity had her hand on the door-knob, but, thus appealed to, she had to turn and answer, as honestly as she could: "Not yet, but you've only been here a week, and it's no use hoping for a rapid improvement."

"No; results have to be measured by

weeks and even by months," Randall agreed. "Don't go yet," he added, so she had to stay while he talked to Mrs. Bradshaw, and examined her. Several times, he asked Verity some question, but scarcely glanced at her as he spoke. When he was leaving, he looked at her directly for the first time. "You've done after-stroke care before?"

"Yes, I worked for six months in a geriatric ward."

"You've done very well so far. We don't need any outside experts yet."

He and Mrs. Hall left, and Verity replaced Mrs. Bradshaw's table, saw that various things were conveniently within reach, and then she left, too.

A little later, she was summoned to Mrs. Hall's office, and given some detailed instructions about Mrs. Bradshaw. "Olga will have to carry them out in the morning," said Mrs. Hall, "but it will be your job during the rest of the day. Olga's a good nurse, but you take a more personal interest in people, and I think that's a help with someone like Mrs. Bradshaw. Dr. Webber thinks she needs a lot of encouragement to keep on trying."

Verity reflected bitterly that Randall obviously preferred to give instructions through a third party, rather than talk to her any more than was absolutely necessary. Although he had praised her work, his voice had been briskly impersonal, and she wondered again what had gone so suddenly and so bleakly wrong. If she knew the cause she might find it easier to bear.

8

ON Wednesday morning, Verity decided to climb the hill behind the church. She knew there was no danger of meeting Randall at that time of day, and while she was so uncertain, she preferred to avoid him. The day was cold and windy, but dry, and she walked quickly, goaded by a desperate desire to keep moving, until she reached the end of the range. Then she stood for some time looking at a wild cold sea, as grey as her own thoughts.

The days seemed leaden, and twice their usual length, but she offered to work on Friday, as she had done the previous week, and because they were short-staffed, her offer was accepted. She had just taken in Colonel Nesbit's tea, and was pouring out his first cup, when Randall appeared

166

in the doorway. A moment later, Verity saw with astonishment that he was accompanied by a complete stranger, a tall, red-haired young woman. He gave Verity a startled glance, as though surprised to see her there, then went across to the other side of the bed.

"I've brought my new partner with me, Colonel. She's just starting work here, so I thought you might like to meet her. Dr. Rowan Fraser, Colonel Nesbit. And this is Verity Lawson."

Dr. Fraser greeted them both in a very friendly manner. She and Colonel Nesbit exchanged a few friendly re-marks, and Randall added: "Rowan is accompanying me on my rounds, so that she can get to know her way among these twisty lanes, and small villages, and I thought it was a good opportunity for her to meet a few of the people here."

They left, and Verity began to help Colonel Nesbit with his tea, while she struggled silently to master her own reactions to the newcomer. "A woman doctor, that will be a change," Colonel Nesbit remarked thoughtfully. "I wonder if she'll be coming here instead of Randall. I hope not. She sounded quite young. About how old is she?"

"I should think about twenty-six, or seven."

"Tell me what she looks like. Is she pretty?"

"Remarkably pretty." Verity had no difficulty in answering that question. She had too vivid a picture of bright sherry-brown eyes, shining dark red hair, and beautiful, expensively casual clothes. She knew that Colonel Nesbit liked to have a detailed picture of people's appearance, so she did her best. "She's tall, probably about five foot seven, or eight, and she has lovely features, bright reddish chestnut hair, and brown eyes."

"But you didn't like her?"

"Do I give that impression?" Verity asked, a little put out. With somewhat painful honesty, she added; "I liked the little I saw of her, but you can't judge people by their looks."

"It certainly isn't safe to do so," he agreed. "Voices are sometimes more revealing than looks. I thought her voice was beautiful, but rather bossy, didn't you?"

Verity answered somewhat at random, still not fully in command of herself, and he turned his head, as though wanting to see her expression. For once, Verity was glad to get away from him. But then she encountered Olga and Ruth, the very last pair she wanted to see. They were standing heads together, talking and laughing, but turned as she came up, and gazed at her with malicious curiosity. "Have you seen Randall's new partner?" asked Olga, and Verity knew that she had deliberately framed her question to emphasise the connection between him and Dr. Fraser.

The conviction that she had been the chief subject of their talk and laughter stiffened her pride, and enabled her to answer quite lightly: "Yes, but only for one minute."

"It's quite a surprise, isn't it?" Olga went on with a knowing smirk. "I'd no idea she was a woman, and such a good-looker, had you?"

"Oh, yes. Randall told me all about her, two or three weeks ago," Verity answered, though not with absolute truth, and went quickly on her way. She felt that she could endure any disappointment, any unhappiness, but other people's curiosity or pity were quite unbearable.

She took Mrs. Bradshaw's tea next, only to find that Randall had been in to see her, as well. "Do you think that new doctor may be coming here, now?" she asked Verity anxiously. "I do hope not. She seemed very pleasant, but I've only just got used to Dr. Webber, and I don't want to have to get to know another doctor. Besides I like him. He never tries to hurry me. I think he's a good doctor, don't you?"

"Very good," Verity agreed. "But

I've no idea which of them will be coming in future. As it's a group of four, we're liable to get any one of them, and they wouldn't have chosen Dr. Fraser unless they thought she was a good doctor too."

Mrs. Bradshaw's questions and comments were repeated by many of the residents, and Verity could still find some pleasure in this proof that Randall was valued and liked. It was his warmth, naturalness and patience that made him so much liked there, even more than his good looks and vitality.

These repeated reminders made it difficult, if not impossible, for her to push the subject to the back of her mind, and keep it there, and she began to feel that the day would never end.

When she got back to her flat, she lit her gas fire, and sat down beside it, trying to fight down the depression that threatened to overwhelm her. In her earlier bafflement, she had told herself that she would find it easier to bear, if only she knew why Randall had changed. Now she knew, and it was no easier. She had sensed an easy friendliness between him and Rowan, and it had brought a stab of savage, primitive pain, almost humiliating in its intensity. Why had she never thought of this obvious explanation? Randall had told her that he had not seen the new partner, but that she was the niece of one of his older partners. That should have suggested that she was probably quite young, but she had concentrated entirely on the fact that Randall would have more time to spend with her. There seemed a bitter irony in that now. She had been living in a dream, only to be awakened to a reality as cold and grey as the winter weather.

She had refused to believe Olga's warnings that Randall liked to take up a new girl, and then to drop her just as quickly. Now, she was forced to wonder if that were really true, but she hated to think any less of him. Rowan Fraser seemed an exceptionally attractive woman, and Verity was generous enough to recognise the presence of qualities which she conspicuously lacked. Rowan Fraser was beautiful, colourful, likeable. With all that she hardly needed brains as well, but she must have plenty to have qualified as a doctor. She seemed to be the picture of a successful career woman, speaking with assurance, knowing how to dress, well used to admiration.

Verity switched on the light, and looked at herself in the mirror, comparing her very ordinary face with Rowan's. Her sparkle and liveliness had faded, so that she looked crushed, pale and quiet, while Rowan was so lovely she wouldn't even need to try. She turned away, and sat down again, telling herself that at least she knew now, and could stop asking questions, and try to come to terms with the facts. To think of Randall with another girl, and one as attractive as Rowan, felt like cutting her heart out, and she fervently wished that she had not told Mrs. Hall that she would stay until the end of February. The sooner she could get away from this place, with all its reminders, the sooner she could begin to forget. She was not sure if she ever could forget Randall, but at least she would try, and the weeks that had seemed so short, now seemed to stretch endlessly before her.

Work had helped to keep miserable thoughts at bay, but now she felt that probably most of the staff knew that she had been seeing a lot of Randall, and had been superseded by the newcomer, and would be speculating about her feelings, some sympathetically, some maliciously. Verity wanted the sympathy no more than the malice, and tried to ignore both and concentrate on her job. She was determined not to inflict her misery on the elderly residents, many of whom had troubles of their own. To speculative and interested glances she presented a front of bright indifference, and no one asked any outright questions. On Sunday afternoon, she heard that Randall had been to Westfield in the morning, alone, and she wondered if he intended to continue doing the country round. On the whole, she would find it a relief if Dr. Fraser did take over.

Verity found that she could be brave enough in company, but she dreaded the prospect of a whole day off on Monday. Having worked on Friday, she could not suggest working on Monday as well. She felt that she was very unlikely to meet Randall up on the hill now, but she could not walk there alone without seeing him much too vividly and painfully, so she filled up the morning with odd jobs, and went shopping in the afternoon. That left her with no occupation for the evening. It was difficult to write cheerful letters home, she felt no impulse to draw, and her thoughts were such miserable company she was glad to return to work next day, and to work overtime again on Friday.

Once back at work, she could feel

that she was in control of herself again, her personal affairs pushed to the back of her mind. Even the routine of the place was a help. She spent a good deal of time with Mrs. Bradshaw. She was quiet and rather reserved, but Verity liked her very much, and determined to do her utmost to help her to return to a more independent life. It was something worthwhile to aim for, and it was just possible that it could be achieved before she left Westfield. She still spent a good deal of time with Colonel Nesbit, too, but felt an unaccustomed uneasiness when she was with him. Even without eyes he sometimes seemed to see things that other people missed. She strained every nerve to seem cheerful with him, but suspected that he knew something was wrong. The fact that he asked nothing only meant that he knew she wanted no questions.

She saw Randall only once at Westfield, and they exchanged no words. That was in some ways a relief to Verity. She did not have to pretend to him, yet it seemed a sad contrast to the past, when he nearly always stopped for a few friendly words. On Friday afternoon, Dr. Fraser came in to see Mrs. Bradshaw while Verity was with her. During her visit, she learnt that Dr. Fraser would be doing that round for the next two or three weeks, because Randall was taking a belated holiday, and had gone to Austria for winter sports. Verity felt that it would be a great relief to have no fear of encountering him for some time.

Although it was a relief, the days seemed flat and endless, with a dull pain underlying all her thoughts and activities. She was glad that she was still working the same shift. It was easier to fill up the morning, knowing that she would be working for the rest of the day, than to find occupation for a long empty evening. On Monday, she went for a walk in the hills, but there were too many reminders there. In the evening, she tried to read a book borrowed from the mobile library, but Randall's face and voice persisted in getting between her and the printed page. She put the book down, and allowed her thoughts to roam freely, remembering all the times she had spent with him, from that first casual invitation to go sight-seeing. She had been well warned, but none of it had done any good. He was simply someone whom she could not help but love, even now when she felt that he had not treated her very kindly. She wished she knew whether he had felt some affection for her, or if she had been just a pleasant girl, good company until a more attractive one appeared.

She returned to work with relief on Tuesday, and continued to work on Fridays. She saw Dr. Fraser several times when she came to Westfield. In some ways, Verity would have liked to dislike her, but could not. She spent less time with some old people than Randall, but she was conscientious, competent, and very friendly.

Then Mrs. Rudd went down with bronchitis again. Now that she and Verity were good friends, she agreed to bed and a doctor without any arguments, and Verity was very glad that Randall was away, with more than half his holiday still to come. Dr. Fraser came in the morning, before Verity had to leave for work, and agreed that she could easily look after Mrs. Rudd, as it was quite a mild attack.

That Friday, Verity had agreed to work a split duty, working morning and evening, with time off in the afternoon. She had started to get tea ready, when she saw Dr. Fraser arriving to see Mrs. Rudd. After letting her in, she went upstairs, turned the kettle out, drew the curtains to shut out the dismal day, and laid a tray for Mrs. Rudd. Then she heard quick steps on the stairs, and Dr. Fraser appeared in the open doorway.

"So that is your flat!" She came into the room, her eyes going round it, curious and friendly. "I'm living with my uncle at present, but I've started looking for a flat of my own. This looks neat and convenient."

"It's not smart, but it is comfortable and convenient," agreed Verity. "Would you like a cup of tea? It would only take a minute or two to get it."

"I would, very much."

While Verity put the kettle on, and got out more crockery, her visitor roamed around, looking at things in a casual and friendly way. Then her eye fell on a pile of sketches Verity had been sorting, and she gave a startled exclamation: "Are these your work?" Verity had tossed the sketches down when she went to open the door, and then forgotten all about them. Dr. Fraser picked the top one up, laughed, and held it out. "That's Mrs. Marshall, isn't it? I hope she was flattered by her portrait, but I doubt it. She looks *very* disapproving."

A small grin hovered around Verity's lips, as she glanced at the sketch. "I drew it from memory, so she hasn't seen it."

"Just as well, I should think. You seem to have quite a portrait gallery here. You don't mind if I look through them?"

Verity agreed, though a little reluctantly. When she poured out the tea, Dr. Fraser sat down, putting the rest of the sketches beside her. "Do call me Rowan here. I think your drawings are amazingly lifelike. I can recognise the people I've met, instantly. Why didn't you go in for art as a career, instead of nursing? You'd have had more freedom, and probably a lot more money."

Verity shook her head. "It isn't easy to earn a living in art, unless you teach, and I'd rather have nursing than that."

"Even in a home for geriatrics? I wouldn't want to deal with old people all the time."

"But I only took that as a temporary job. I'm leaving at the end of February, and I'll be very sorry to part from some of the old people at Westfield."

"Yes, you seem to like them, if your sketches are anything to go by." Rowan finished her tea, and picked up the bunch of drawings. A few moments later she gave another laughing exclamation: "That's Randall to the life!" She held up a sketch, and Verity saw with dismay that one of her private collection had somehow got mixed in with the others. "And this one is part of Easterbrook Farm, isn't it?"

"Yes, but I drew both from memory, so they're probably not very good."

"Oh, I think this one of Randall is excellent. It even conveys that impression of casual untidiness." Rowan laughed again, affectionate laughter, Verity thought. "A brilliant mind, but a sartorial disgrace! What Randall really needs is some ambition. He ought to specialise in geriatrics. The old people at Westfield love him, and seem to think I'm a very poor substitute. They're always asking when he'll be back. He's wasted in a country practice."

"But you've come to work in a country practice yourself," Verity pointed out.

"That's not for lack of ambition. I've had to learn my limitations, and I know that I'm just good average. But Randall isn't. He has a first-class brain, and could go far. Don't you agree?"

"Yes; but why should he change, if he's doing good work here, and is happy doing it?"

"Because it's a waste," said Rowan very emphatically. She began to put on her coat. "I've enjoyed looking at your drawings, but if I could draw as well as that, I wouldn't be content with a nurse's pay. I think *you* could do with more ambition, too." Her friendly smile robbed the words of any possible offence. "I'll be in to see Mrs. Rudd on Tuesday. I don't suppose Randall will be back then."

"When is he coming back?"

"Wednesday or Thursday. His brother's getting married next Friday, and Randall's best man, so he'll have to be back by then. The sooner the better, as far as I'm concerned."

Rowan was probably referring to the

practice, but Verity sensed that work was not her only reason for wanting Randall back. Looking at her lively face, at her bright sherry-brown eyes, and the shining red hair mingling with her fur collar, she felt a piercing stab of envy. She had meant to ask Rowan which of them would be doing the country round, but she could not trust her voice. She would know soon enough.

Rowan left, and Verity made fresh tea for Mrs. Rudd, and took it down to her. She went back upstairs and cleared away their tea-things. Somewhat against her own will, she found that she liked Rowan even more than at first. She was confidently aware of her own good looks, yet not conceited. It was hardly surprising that Randall found her very attractive, and she was quite sure that Rowan reciprocated that feeling. Her instant recognition of one bit of Easterbrook Farm, suggested that Randall had taken her there more than once, in the short time before he went away. With an effort, she thrust tormenting thought from her, and began to get ready to return to Westfield. Once there, she was quickly caught up in the busy routine of the place, and could at least partially forget her own troubles, but a dull ache, a feeling of irreparable loss, never entirely left her.

9

WHEN Verity took tea to Mrs. Marshall's room that Sunday, she saw that all her relations were assembled there. Ralph returned her smile, but it struck her that he looked somewhat embarrassed. When she went out, she realised that it was four or five weeks since she had seen him, except visiting his aunt, and she had not heard anything from him in that time. She had been too absorbed in thoughts about Randall to notice this, but now she asked herself what was wrong with her that no one wanted to remain friends with her for long. She paused in front of a mirror, and considered herself seriously. The lively vitality of her face was quenched. She decided that she looked colourless and drab, and it was no wonder that men quickly lost interest. She gave a wry and slightly defiant grin at her reflection, and passed on. Perhaps Ralph also had found a more attractive and colourful girl, but it was not really important to her.

Monday was windy and blustery, but bright for early December, so Verity decided to go for a walk across the hill, in the early afternoon. As Randall would be returning in two or three days, it was the last time she could walk there, and feel sure that she would not meet him. The grass was wet, and her feet were soon almost as wet, but she kept on walking. Two-thirds of the way across the hill, she climbed up a slope, and saw two riders coming towards her along the path.

She would have known Randall anywhere, and Rowan's bright hair made her equally easy to recognise. Her first instinct was to dodge down the hill, but they must have seen her, and she was not near any of the side paths. If she turned back, they would soon overtake her. She did the only reasonable thing, walked steadily on, but her heart was knocking on her ribs, and she would have given a good deal to avoid the encounter. Randall's horse checked, and she suspected that he had recognised her, and did not want to meet her, but Rowan came on at the same brisk pace. She reined in her horse as she drew level with Verity.

"Isn't it marvellous weather for December?" Verity agreed, and then Rowan went on: "One of us will be coming to see Mrs. Rudd tomorrow, but I'm not sure which. Randall's got a few days of his holiday left, but he says he may start work tomorrow, and take them later."

Randall came slowly up to them. He gave Verity a quick and impersonal greeting. His cool almost formal voice seemed to twist her heart, and she gave up any idea of asking what sort of a holiday he had had. She could not trust her voice not to betray her, particularly with Rowan listening. It was a relief when Rowan gathered her reins, saying:

"Well, my time is limited, so I'd better get on." She rode on with a gay wave of her hand, Randall just behind.

Verity stood looking after them. Rowan's chestnut hair seemed to catch every gleam of the winter sunshine. Randall quickly drew level with her, and they went on at a fast trot, until they disappeared down the next slope of the hill. Verity made for the nearest side path down the hill. It would mean a longer walk, but she could not bear to meet them again, as they came back. She walked blindly, absorbed in her thoughts. She was remembering an early meeting with Randall on the hill, when he had said that he would teach her to ride, if he had more time. He had more time now, but Rowan was his chosen companion, and she was already a good rider.

She wondered why he had come back from his holiday sooner than expected. Perhaps Rowan was the reason. He had not yet started work, but he had obviously wasted no time before arranging to meet her. Tears stung Verity's eyes, then began to trickle down her cheeks. She wiped them impatiently away, but they continued to fall, to her own furious annoyance. She never cried easily, even as a child, and felt ashamed of being unable to control her tears now. No one else had ever had such power to make her feel desolate. The thought of Randall, and of her own hopes and dreams, was still a raw aching wound. She had told herself that she had learnt to accept it, but the sight of him again, with Rowan, had brought it back in all its first rawness. Colonel Nesbit was right when he said she was too easily made glad, she told herself bitterly. And why had she chosen to walk on the hill today? She would never go there again, for the rest of her stay, she told herself.

The sunshine vanished as she walked, and the light was beginning to fade. She glanced at her watch, and quickened her pace, not wanting to be late getting Mrs. Rudd's tea. But once tea was over and washed up, the rest of the evening stretched emptily before her. She found herself wondering what Rowan was doing, whether she had to take evening surgery, or was having an evening out with Randall. Against her own will, her imagination took complete control of her mind, creating one scene after another, with Rowan and Randall together, in the places where she had been with Randall.

By morning, Verity was feeling apprehensive about which doctor would come to see Mrs. Rudd. She thought Randall might well prefer not to come, but if he had started work again, and if he intended to stick to his old round, then Mrs. Rudd would be on his list. It was a great relief when Rowan arrived in the middle of the morning, and decided that Mrs. Rudd would need no more visits. Being a friendly and talkative girl, she went on to tell Verity that Randall had started work that morning, and that it had been decided that he would continue doing the country round. He liked it, and she did not, but she was doing it for one more morning, because he was rather tied up with other things in Bretton.

Verity listened with mixed feelings. Many of the old people at Westfield would be delighted to see Randall back, but it would have been easier for her, if Rowan had taken his place there. She could not help wondering if Randall had left that morning's visits to Rowan, because he wanted to avoid meeting and talking to her except at Westfield, where there were plenty of other people, and it was easy to be formal.

She saw nothing of Randall in the next few days, but gathered that he had been to Westfield one morning. She worked all day on Friday, preferring to be fully occupied. During a quiet spell in the evening she read to Colonel Nesbit, but after a while he stopped her.

"If you've time to stay and talk to me, then do, but you sound tired, and

I'm sure you've read enough for now," he said kindly. "I think you're over-working. How long is it since you took two days off in any one week?"

"I don't remember." Verity admitted. "But I enjoy my work here, so — "

She broke off in mid-sentence, as the door opened, and Randall came in. He looked as surprised as she felt, hesi-tated, then walked over to the colonel. "I'm late finishing, on account of Bill's wedding," he told him. "You said you wanted to hear how it went off, so I thought I'd come and tell you about it now, as I've finished for the day, I hope."

As he spoke, Verity shut her book, and got to her feet, intending to make a quick, quiet exit, but before she could do so, the colonel put out his better hand to detain her. "I'll be delighted to hear all about it, but first I want you to back me up in something else. I've just been telling Verity she's doing too much. It's weeks since she's had more than one day off each week. It's too much."

Hot colour flooded over Verity's neck and face. Randall looked at her directly for the first time, his eyes narrowed and intent, "Surely it isn't necessary to work that much overtime?" he asked.

"We are short of staff, so Mrs. Hall is glad of the extra time. There's not very much to do this weather, and I am *not* overworked or put upon," she answered firmly.

"I don't agree," said Colonel Nesbit equally firmly. "If there's nothing to do here, why not go and see your friend in Oxford?"

"Perhaps after Christmas, but not now."

Colonel Nesbit released her hand, so she went quickly to the door, but before she reached it, Randall's voice stopped her again. "I've been wanting to tell you that I've been surprised and pleased at the amount of progress Mrs. Bradshaw has made these last few weeks. I think she owes it a good deal to you."

Pleased yet embarrassed by this

praise, Verity glanced at him quickly, then away again. "I think it's mainly due to her own determination."

"She says she could never have persevered so much without your support and encouragement. I've suggested a visiting physiotherapist, but she says she'd rather just have your help. If she feels like that, then I think that's probably best for the present."

He turned to Colonel Nesbit, and Verity made her escape, a prey to a very confused blend of feelings. While she was pleased by Randall's praise of her work, she knew that it was the doctor speaking, not the man. She was soon too busy for connected thought, but half an hour later, she was told that Mrs. Hall wanted to see her in her sitting-room, as soon as she was free. Puzzled by the summons, but not apprehensive, because she got on well with Mrs. Hall, she finished what she was doing, then went to her sitting-room. Mrs. Hall put down her book, and invited her to sit down. "I've just been talking to Randall Webber. Or rather, he's been talking to me. He says I'm overworking you, expecting you to do too much overtime."

The colour crept up to Verity's cheeks again. "It was something Colonel Nesbit said to him. I've not been complaining. After all, I *offered* to do it."

"Yes, and I've been very glad to accept, but one can take a willing worker too much for granted." Mrs. Hall regarded her thoughtfully. "I'm not sure that he isn't right. I hadn't realised how long it is since you had two days off, and you do look tired. From now on you must take your full time off. No," she over-rode Verity's attempt at protest, "that's final, for the present. January and February are the worst months for having people ill, and staff off sick too. I may have to ask you to work overtime then, so it's silly to overdo it now. After all, working your present shift, you have no free evenings except on your days off. Most young nurses want more than that."

Verity sensed, or perhaps just imagined, a slight question in the last sentence. She wondered if Mrs. Hall knew that she had spent a good deal of her free time in Randall's company, but did so no longer. She answered as lightly as she could: "I'd rather be off in the mornings. There are disadvantages to living in a small village with no transport of your own." For the second time that evening, she was glad to escape.

About an hour later, she walked slowly home through a starry, frosty night. She had been startled and shaken to find that Randall had taken enough notice of Colonel Nesbit's remarks to talk to Mrs. Hall about her. In fact, she would much rather have continued working on Fridays, but that did not make her any less grateful for the thought that had prompted his action. She felt that she understood him a little better now. Since Randall changed towards her, she had been quite unable to decide whether he had been a little in love with her, or if it had all been a combination of ignorance and imagination on her part. Tonight, she had sensed a certain embarrassment in his manner. She thought he would not have come to Colonel Nesbit's room, if he had known that she was there, and that he would have preferred to retreat, if he could. Yet he had prolonged their time together by praising her work, and then gone out of his way to discuss her hours with Mrs. Hall. It seemed to Verity that he had been attracted to her, perhaps only a little, then Rowan had appeared on the scene, and he had fallen really in love with her. She felt that his present coolness was not due to any unfriendly feeling, only to embarrassment, because he knew that she was still in love with him, and perhaps blamed himself for having encouraged her.

Verity did not blame him. He had made no promises, never suggested anything except that he enjoyed her company. It was not his fault if, through inexperience and wishful thinking, she had imagined far more than had ever existed. Nor was it his fault that he had fallen in love with Rowan. How did anyone stop themselves falling in love? She did not know. She had done it herself, completely and recklessly, and now felt as though she had lost a part of herself.

Christmas was less than two weeks away now, and this added in a small degree to Verity's difficulties. Olga went round Westfield boasting about all the parties to which she had been invited, the festivities in which she would be taking part, and she was continually asking Verity about her plans, then giving knowing looks and malicious comments about her total lack of any dates. Verity tried to explain this by the fact that she would be working over the Christmas holiday, so that the married staff could have more time off, but she felt that it was a very thin explanation. Many of the old people asked similar questions, but with much kinder motives. Verity hated to think that she was an object of pity, and her thoughts turned to Ralph. She had seen nothing of him for quite a long time, and had not really missed his friendship. She had been too unhappy to worry about a minor loss, but now she found herself thinking that even one date with Ralph would have been a slight salve to her pride, and some defence against Olga. She wondered again why he had dropped her so abruptly, when he had been too possessive at their last meeting. The most likely explanation seemed the same as with Randall, a new and better girl.

She had looked forward to an English Christmas but felt now that she would be glad when it was over, then told herself that such an attitude was unfair to the old people at Westfield. Many of them genuinely looked forward to Christmas, but some of them were alone in the world, or, like Mrs.

Marshall, had only relatives who were more devoted to their possessions than to them. Ten days before Christmas, she received two unexpected invitations. Mrs. Farley, mother of Martin, the boy who fell off his bike, asked her to join them for dinner on Christmas Day, and the senior nurse, Mrs. Grey, gave her an open invitation to join her family any time over the holiday. Verity was grateful, but had to refuse both, because of the hours she would be working. In order to free as many staff as possible, she had agreed to work a split duty each day, from Christmas Eve to Boxing Day, working in the morning, with a few hours off in the afternoon, then returning for the evening.

A third and even more unexpected invitation she did accept. Martin Farley's older brother, Richard, was home from the university. Verity had met him out walking with Martin, and they had become fairly friendly, but she was surprised when he asked her to go with him to a New Year's Dance in Bretton. After an initial hesitation, she accepted, she was not quite sure why. She did not particularly want to go, but she would be off then, and she liked Richard, and perhaps Olga's spiteful remarks and comments had something to do with it. It was pleasant to feel that she was liked, and her company wanted, by someone, even if he were not the person who really mattered. Now that she had got things clearer in her mind, it was some consolation to think that Randall avoided her because of embarrassment, or because he felt that it was the kindest way, and not because he disliked her.

She knew that she was well liked by many of the residents of Westfield. Mrs. Salter returned the week before Christmas, walking surprisingly well with the help of a walking aid, and delighted to be back again. Verity was almost as pleased to see her there, and brought her up-to-date with news and gossip. She also told her something about Mrs. Bradshaw. "She's still nervous about walking, and won't try on her own," she told her. "I think she'd feel encouraged to see how well you can walk, after having to learn all over again."

Mrs. Salter was sociable and friendly, and delighted at the prospect of being of some use to another woman. Mrs. Bradshaw was just the opposite, rather shy, and very sensitive about her disabilities, especially her speech difficulties. But Verity talked to her about Mrs. Salter, until she agreed to meet her, and then they became good friends. Mrs. Salter even persuaded Mrs. Bradshaw to sample the general sitting-room, and get to know some of the other residents.

Having spent two Christmases working in a hospital, Verity had become accustomed to receiving small presents from grateful patients, but she was still startled by the number she received at Westfield, handkerchieves and scarves enough to last her for some time, chocolates, talc and bathsalts, far more than she could possibly get through in the next two months. Touched and grateful, but a little overwhelmed, she decided that she would have to leave them with Amanda, after she left Westfield.

Colonel Nesbit gave chocolate or book tokens to each of the nursing staff. When Verity thanked him for her book token he said: "I have something more personal for you, only I'm not giving it to you just yet. But I would like to show it to you. Would you pass me that small red box from my table." The small leather box usually sat on the table, within his reach, and Verity had sometimes wondered about it. Colonel Nesbit opened it with his left hand, and showed her a fine diamond and ruby ring. "My wife's engagement ring," he told her. "I like to keep it here, because a photograph means nothing to me now. I want you to have it some day, but not just yet. If

I'd had a grand-daughter, I would have given it to her. These last few months, you've given me as much kindness and as much pleasure as any grand-daughter could, so I want you to have it."

"I don't know what to say," exclaimed Verity.

"Don't say anything, I'm very glad to think of your having it. You see, I've no near relations, so most of my money will go to favourite charities, but I'd far rather give something as personal as this to someone I know and like. Mind, you must feel free to do as you like with it, wear it, or sell it for something you'd like better, like seeing a little more of the world."

"I'd never sell it."

"That must be just as you want. You might even wear it as your own engagement ring some day. I'm not superstitious, but ours was a very happy marriage, and you never know, it might bring you luck as well."

Verity could not trust herself to

comment on this. She put her hand over his, and he turned his head slightly, as though wanting to see her face. Then he added: "We all have trials and disappointments. Sometimes they seem more than we can bear, but the stars shine still."

"You can still say that, tied here in one room, unable to see the stars or anything else?" she said, marvelling.

"Oh, yes. They still shine for me in thoughts of the past, and the future. I won't need this ring then, and I'd like to think of your wearing it. Put it away now." More briskly, he added: "There's a very true saying I once heard, however long you weep, you have to blow your nose in the end."

Verity was surprised into a real laugh. "You're probably right, though I could never have said it half so neatly." She dropped a warm, impulsive kiss on his cheek, and carried his tray away, wondering how much he had guessed about herself and Randall.

Mrs. Rudd had gone to stay with a

sister over Christmas. When Verity returned late that night, the house felt very dark and cold. She lit her gas fire, and made some coffee, and then her thoughts wandered to Randall, and how he had spent Christmas Day, probably with his family, but was Rowan with them too? Then she caught up her wandering thoughts, telling herself that self-pity was much too easy. She would not go through life heartsick for what she could not have. Her talk with Colonel Nesbit had put new heart into her, and she decided that it was time she thought less about the past, and more about the future. It was foolish and wasteful not to make the most of what she had, and especially this year in England. She had only just over two months here. She had intended to follow it with a tour of the West Country, before looking for another job. Now, she felt that she would rather go farther away. She would go and stay with Amanda for a while, and look for a new job, perhaps in or near Oxford, but preferably even farther afield, Wales, or the north of England.

Olga and Ruth had both had a few days holiday around Christmas. They returned determined to tell everyone how they had spent the time, and what plans they had made for the New Year. Their condescending pity for Verity's dull Christmas stung her into saying that she was going to a New Year's Eve dance with Richard Farley. Olga looked very taken aback, and said, with a faint trace of envy, "That's the smartest New Year's Eve dance in Bretton." Then she recovered her usual form, and added: "I believe Randall Webber went to it last year. He'll probably take Rowan Fraser there this year." Seeing Verity's face, Olga gave a smug smile, and walked off.

Verity had given very little thought to the dance. Perhaps that was why it had never occurred to her that she might see Randall there. She fervently hoped that she would not, and felt even less inclined for a dance than before. She had two possible dresses, both having associations she tried not to remember. The green and white one, bought in Bretton, was the prettier, so she chose that. She surveyed herself critically, a slim, neatly-made girl, with brown hair, a short tilted nose, and expressive eyes. Well enough, she decided, but ordinary compared with Rowan's bright and lovely colouring. Then she did her best to dismiss Rowan and Randall from her thoughts, and make herself a pleasant companion for Richard.

Soon after they began dancing together, she saw Ralph. He looked surprised, but gave her a friendly smile. Ten minutes later, she saw Randall and Rowan dancing together. They made a very noticeable pair, and Richard soon asked: "Do you know who that red-haired girl is, dancing with Randall Webber?"

"His new partner, Dr. Rowan Fraser."

"I'd heard the new doctor was a woman, but I'd no idea she was such a dazzler."

"She's nice, as well as good-looking," said Verity, generously.

Rowan was wearing a patterned dress of russet and gold on a background of darkest nigger-brown. It was a perfect match for her red-brown hair, making her look sophisticated and colourful, and making Verity feel even more ordinary. A little later, she danced with Ralph, and although he was perfectly friendly she thought he seemed faintly embarrassed again, and looked at her a little oddly. The last time they had been together he had spoken of getting in touch, arranging another outing, and she guessed that he felt awkward about not having done so. She danced with one or two people she had met at the party to which Ralph had taken her, but mainly with Richard, and she did her best to enjoy the dance, or at least to make Richard think she enjoyed it.

They broke off to get drinks and something to eat, and as they made their way back to the dance floor, she came face to face with Randall and

Rowan, for the first time that evening. Rowan had stopped, and was fiddling with the buckle of her sandal. She straightened up as Verity and Richard came along.

"I've found a flat, just what I wanted," she told Verity. "I moved in ten days ago." She began to describe the flat in some detail, but Verity listened with only half her attention, noting that Randall and Richard were talking as old friends or acquaintances. When Rowan paused, Randall introduced Richard, and he immediately asked her for a dance.

They moved away together, and Randall and Verity were alone. Silence fell like a stone between them, and Verity knew that he was wondering how to get out of asking her to dance, without being downright rude. She glanced at him quickly, saw that his eyes were cool and wary, and embarrassment made her rush into speech on the first neutral topic that came into her head.

"I suppose you're very busy, at this time of year?" she asked.

"Yes, very. There's a good deal of whooping-cough around, and an increasing amount of 'flu since Christmas, I hope it doesn't spread to Westfield."

"Oh, so do I," exclaimed Verity, forgetting some of her self-consciousness at this thought.

Some more people came along from the buffet. Two stopped to speak to Randall, and she made her escape, wondering if he could be half as relieved to see her go as she was to get away. She wanted to dance with him as little as he wanted to dance with her, but it hurt her to feel that they were no more than uneasy strangers now.

She and Richard stayed until the dance finished. She saw Randall several times in passing, but they did not speak again. Richard parted from her with a very friendly kiss, and good wishes for the New Year. Verity returned both, but could not believe in anything very good for herself in the near future. When she was alone, the unhappiness she had been keeping at bay for the last few hours rolled over and engulfed her. She closed her eyes, trying to blot out the image of Randall's face, aloof and unsmiling, but it was replaced by a series of vivid pictures which seemed to pass before her closed eyes, of all the other times when they had been together as friends. Why could they not be friends still, instead of uneasy strangers? There was a yawning gap in her life that only one person could fill, and until she could get right away from him she would remain just as helplessly in love. Two months would probably pass quite quickly, but at that moment it seemed a very long time indeed.

10

A COUPLE of days after the dance, Olga and Ruth were both off with 'flu. They probably caught it at one of their many parties, thought Verity, rather uncharitably, and hoped they had not passed it on to any of the old people. During the next week several more nurses went down with the complaint, and a number of the elderly residents caught it. That meant that the nursing-home was very understaffed, just when they most need a full staff. The remaining nurses, including Verity, worked very long hours. She took no days off, and, although only a junior, she was sometimes in charge of several very sick people. Randall was in every day, and sometimes more than once a day, and they were both far too busy with other people to have time for embarrassment

214

or self-consciousness. Verity knew that Randall approved of her as a nurse, and she found it quite a consolation that they could still be good partners at work.

By mid-January about half the residents were in bed with 'flu, several of them very ill, and more than a third of the staff were off with it, including Mrs. Hall. Verity hoped that Olga and Ruth, having been the first to contract it, would soon be back, but she was sure that they would both stay off as long as they could. She was thankful that Colonel Nesbit and Mrs. Bradshaw were among those who had escaped it, so far. She could give no extra time to Mrs. Bradshaw now, but she rose to the crisis, telling Verity that she would somehow manage to wash and dress and eat without assistance, and began to move about alone for the first time, with a walking aid.

Mrs. Marshall was down with 'flu. She was not seriously ill, but Verity found her one of her most difficult patients, demanding, fractious, and impossible to please. She kept on reminding herself that it was far more uncomfortable and painful for Mrs. Marshall to lie in bed all day than it was for some of the others, and so managed to stay helpful and good-humoured with her. Once or twice, she caught an expression of candid dislike in her eyes, and Verity decided that she was one of those people who resented the youth and health of others, even while she relied upon it.

Randall worked himself unsparingly, and seemed immune to 'flu. At the height of the outbreak, Verity watched him one afternoon as he examined Mrs. Marshall, liking his skilled, gentle hands, and the way he concentrated completely on the person he was with. He glanced up to ask her a question, found her eyes fixed on him, and looked away abruptly, his question unasked. Verity was angry with herself for allowing personal feelings to intrude, wrenched her gaze away, and a few moments later answered him as quickly and composedly as usual.

They left Mrs. Marshall's room, but at the door of the next patient's room, he stopped, and asked, rather abruptly: "Do you find Mrs. Marshall a very difficult patient?"

"Since she's had 'flu, yes," Verity admitted. "Why? Does it show?"

"Only in that patience seemed rather an effort, for once."

"Oh! I'm sorry, but I'm afraid the real difficulty is that she dislikes me."

Randall said nothing, but stood looking at her for a few moments with an expression that Verity thought very peculiar indeed. Then he opened the door of the room. When he had seen all the sick people in her section, he gave one or two final directions, then asked: "How long is it since you took any time off?"

"I don't remember, but we've got to get through the extra work somehow, and it won't be for long. Some of the nurses who got it first will be coming back, so we should soon be over the worst."

"I know, I know, but it's still possible to take on too much," he answered, then moved quickly away.

Verity stood looking after him for a few moments, thinking that it was the first time for weeks that he had spoken to her in anything like his old fashion. As far as his advice was concerned, it seemed rather like the pot calling the kettle black. She didn't believe he had had a half day off since the start of the outbreak. He seemed charged with tireless energy, but today his eyes had looked tired. A wave of passionate love and longing swept through her heart, but she hurried back to work, telling herself that she had no time to waste.

The residents differed widely in their reactions to the difficult conditions. Some complained bitterly because they got a little less attention than usual, but others were very helpful, and enjoyed feeling that they were of use. Mrs. Salter had a mild attack of 'flu, at the start of the outbreak, and was now hobbling cheerfully around with her walking aid, asking what odd jobs she could do to help. Mrs. Hall, who had had quite a sharp attack, started working part-time, and expressed her gratitude to the nurses who had been carrying on.

"Don't try to do too much too soon," Verity advised her. "I don't mind doing extra, and I never get 'flu."

Gradually, the nurses who had been off ill began to return, including Olga and Ruth, very belatedly. By mid-February, three old people had died, but most of the others had recovered, or were recovering, and most of the staff were back.

Mrs. Hall ordered Verity to take a day off, her first that year. During the last six weeks she had had little time to brood. She had dealt with each hour and day as it came, refusing to think about tiredness, but now that the pressure had relaxed, overwork and fatigue seemed to have caught up with her. She decided that she needed some fresh air, and set off to climb the hill.

It was a typical February day, not actually raining, but grey and rather miserable, and Verity's mood matched the grey chill of the weather. She had only another two and a half weeks at Westfield, and although she had longed to get away, she had begun to realise that leaving would be a painful wrench. She had become very attached to some of the people there. She knew Colonel Nesbit would miss her, but she thought she would miss him at least as much, if not more. During the 'flu epidemic she had had an excellent working relationship with Randall, and felt that they had come a little closer together again. Life might be easier away from him, but she hated to contemplate the thought of never seeing him again.

It seemed a very long climb to the top of the hill. When she finally came out on to the open hillside, a wave of exhaustion and dizziness swept over her, and she sat down abruptly on one of the rocky outcrops. Her dizziness soon passed, but by then she was shivering in the cold wind that swept across the hillside. She told herself that she must walk on, or go back, but could not summon up enough energy to do either. She was still debating the matter when she became aware of the sound of hoof-beats approaching. She turned, and saw two riders cantering along the track, both bare-headed, one with red hair, one black, both very recognisable. She watched, hoping that they would turn before they reached the end of the track, but still they came on. She decided to go back down the path, and got to her feet, only to find that her head was swimming, and her legs felt like jelly.

"I say, are you all right?" Rowan asked a few moments later, reining in her horse beside her. "You certainly don't look it."

Randall slid from his horse, and his hands shot out to hold her, and steady her. He gave her one sharp,

221

comprehensive glance, and pronounced: "You've got 'flu."

"I can't have," Verity protested indignantly. "I never get 'flu."

A flash of amusement crossed his face. "There's always a first time," he remarked mildly. "But whatever possessed you to climb all the way up here when you were feeling groggy? And on a day like this?"

"I was feeling all right when I started. At least, I think I was."

"Do you think you can walk home?" asked Rowan. "You look all in."

"Of course I can. It's all downhill."

"None the less, I think four legs might be better than two, and much quicker," said Randall. He took his arm from Verity's shoulder, swung himself up into the saddle, and then before she had realised his intention, he reached down, and swung her up in front of him, with effortless ease. It was done so quickly that she had neither time nor breath to protest. "If you're not very comfortable, it won't be for long," he told her, gathering up the reins.

They rode a little way along the track, then he turned down a side path, telling Rowan: "You go straight back to the farm. I won't be much behind you." The path led to a lane, still descending quite steeply. Randall rode fairly slowly, and they were both silent, Verity too shaken to speak, and very conscious of his arm holding her close.

When they reached a level road his pace quickened, and she let her head rest against him, finding a bitter-sweet comfort in the contact. But she lifted it sharply when he turned in at the Westfield gateway.

"Why are you going here?" she asked. "I thought you were going to my flat."

"Do you want to give Mrs. Rudd 'flu, as well? I think that would be very unwise. Much better to see if Mrs. Hall has a vacant room."

"I've got everything I'm likely to want in my flat, so Mrs. Rudd need not come near me. Mrs. Hall has enough on her shoulders already, and I don't want to be any trouble."

Without even bothering to answer her protests, Randall pulled up his horse, dismounted, twisted the reins around a handy tree branch, then lifted her from the saddle, and carried her indoors. Verity decided she might as well give up useless protest. He set her down in the hall, just as Mrs. Hall appeared. She glanced from one to the other, and asked: "What's wrong now?"

"'Flu I think," Randall answered. "Quite a nasty attack by the look of her, and that's something of a problem. If I take her to her flat, there's no one to look after her except an elderly woman who's had bronchitis twice already this winter. She's escaped the 'flu so far, and I'd rather she didn't get it now, so I wondered if you had a room vacant."

"I always keep one for emergencies, or residents' visitors. She can have that."

Verity decided that it was about time she had some say in the matter. "If I go to bed for a couple of days, I shall be quite all right. I can easily get hot drinks for myself, so Mrs. Rudd needn't come near me. I don't want — "

"To be any trouble," Randall interrupted. "That seems to be your theme song! You looked after Mrs. Rudd when she was ill, so she'd probably insist on looking after you now. Just take a good look at yourself, and you'll see why. Get her off to bed, Mrs. Hall, and take no notice. I've left my horse on your lawn, so I'd better go now. I'll take a look at her later, along with my other patients."

He departed, and Mrs. Hall laughed. "Randall certainly never wastes time. Stop worrying, Verity. You'll be no nuisance, and I owe you a lot more for all the extra work you've been doing. I can lend you a few things, too, and later on one of the girls can collect some of your own for you." She took her to the bedroom, then went to fetch a night-dress, slippers, and a dressing-gown, and promised to ring up Mrs.

Rudd and explain. "Make out a list of things you'll want, and I'll send someone for them. And it won't be Olga," she added reassuringly, revealing a surprising knowledge about staff relationships.

It did not worry Verity that the borrowed garments had probably belonged to some previous resident, now dead. She undressed, without bothering to take Randall's advice to look at herself, and was surprisingly glad to subside into bed. Someone brought her a hot drink she did not really want, and some time later Randall came in.

"You've got a very high temperature, and a nasty dose of 'flu, coming on top of all that overwork," he told her.

"You can just stay there, and stop worrying about being a nuisance. Mrs. Hall is very willing to have you here."

"I know," Verity agreed. "She's been very kind."

Randall paused, looking down at her. "I'm glad to see that you can still smile, even though it isn't a very good smile, far from your best." He stroked the curve of her cheek gently with his finger, his keen blue eyes softening. It was a gentle, curiously tender gesture, and Verity gazed up at him, her eyes full of uncertainties. Then, abruptly, without another word, he was gone. She put her hand on her cheek, where he had touched it, and kept it there. She simply could not understand his sudden changes of mood, but at least, she told herself, he still liked her.

For four days, Verity wanted nothing except peace and quiet and a few drinks. Colonel Nesbit sent her a bunch of lovely roses, and Randall visited her briefly each day. On the fifth day when she was beginning to feel a much livelier interest in the world, Rowan appeared instead, and Verity was surprised into saying: "Randall's not got 'flu, has he?"

"No, he seems immune to all such ordinary weaknesses," Rowan laughed. "He's taking a half day off. The epidemic's nearly over, so we can all have more time off now." She examined Verity, then said: "Your temperature's practically back to normal. You can get up for a few hours tomorrow, if you like."

"Of course I'd like to. And then I can go home the next day."

"Talk to Randall about that. He'll be in tomorrow, to see his remaining patients here. But don't be in too big a hurry. You've had a very nasty dose. I had it, too, earlier on, went back to work too soon, and then had to take a few more days off, which helped no one."

Verity got up after breakfast next day, and was annoyed to find that her legs still felt uncomfortably like jelly. But she told Mrs. Hall very firmly that she would go home next morning. "That depends on Randall," Mrs. Hall answered.

"I can manage perfectly well. I've only had 'flu. I've been here nearly a week, and I know how long your waiting list is."

228

"But I keep this room for emergencies, and another day or two is of no importance."

Verity was still up when Randall came to see her later in the morning, and she repeated her wish to leave the next day.

"Not tomorrow," he said at once. "Yes, I know Mrs. Hall has other uses for the room, but one day is neither here nor there. I'll be in again on Tuesday, about midday, and when I've finished here, I'm taking you to Easterbrook for a week." Surprise left Verity speechless, and he went on quickly: "Now be sensible. You've been quite ill, on top of weeks of overwork, and you'll get over it much faster there than trying to cope with things like shopping here. There's only Nigel at home, now that Bill's married, and my mother says she'll enjoy having some extra company."

"It's very kind of her," began Verity, then paused, suddenly feeling infuriatingly weak and close to tears.

"I've told you, she'll enjoy your company," he said brusquely, going over to the door. "Around twelve, Tuesday, so be ready."

He left, and Verity mopped eyes that had become blurred with tears. She was not quite sure what brought them there, gratitude for Randall's unexpected kindness, or regrets for all the laughter, warmth, and understanding that she had thought they shared. Her feelings about a week at Easterbrook Farm were very mixed, but she certainly felt some pleasure at the prospect, even if only because she owed it to Randall's active kindness. She felt it was typical of him. He was full of small thoughtful kindnesses, which surprised by their unexpectedness, so she did not delude herself by thinking that she was in any way special. She was alone and unwell, in a strange country, and that was all. But perhaps he did have a little extra kindness for her still, she thought, remembering the curiously gentle touch of his finger on her cheek. That personal note had not been repeated, and she thought she was very unlikely to see much, if anything, of him, during her stay at the farm.

Later on, more practical thoughts began to surface. When she returned from Easterbrook, February would be nearly over, and she had planned to leave Westfield at the end of that month, but that would be a very poor return for Mrs. Hall's kindness. She thought it over, and went to see Mrs. Hall immediately after breakfast next morning, and told her what was worrying her.

"No one supposes that you *wanted* to get 'flu," answered Mrs. Hall, looking amused. "In fact, Randall said you'd probably be off for another fortnight, or ten days at least." Looking at Verity's dismayed expression, she added: "I haven't got anyone to replace you, so if you'd care to stay on for another month, I'd be very glad, but you're not under any obligation."

"I think I am. I'll stay for another month, as long as I can keep on my flat. I'm thinking of walking down there now, to collect some clothes to take with me to the farm."

"It's ten minutes walk to the village, and then you'd have to carry them back up the hill. And it's raining. I don't think that's a good idea. There are plenty of people here with cars. I'll ask one of them to run you down there. It won't take you long to pack your things?"

"Hardly any time. I travel light. Can I go in and see Colonel Nesbit and Mrs. Bradshaw tomorrow, before I go? I can't possibly infect them by then, can I?" Mrs. Hall agreed to that. After lunch, Mrs. Grey ran her down to her flat. Verity packed some extra clothes, and Mrs. Rudd agreed very readily to her keeping the flat on for an extra month. Next morning, she took in Colonel Nesbit's breakfast, and thanked him for his roses.

"This is a pleasant surprise. The days

have seemed twice as long without you," he told her, adding: "But it's time I got used to that."

"Not just yet. I'm going to spend a week at Easterbrook Farm. After that, I'll be back, and I'm staying for an extra month, until the end of March."

"That's good news. Not that I'd ever wish to tie you down. You should see something of the world while you're young, as I did. It's a very different world now, though. Have you decided where you'll go from here?"

"Not yet, but wherever it is, I'll write to you regularly," she promised, "and tell you all about it. Someone will read the letters to you. You know, you say that you'll miss me, but I think I'll miss you more. In some ways," Verity said slowly, "I don't want to leave here, and that's mostly you. Knowing you has been quite an experience. You've taught me so many things, about other people and about myself. I shall never think in quite the same way again. I think you have a gift for stretching the imagination."

He smiled: "You've sometimes said that I pay nice compliments. Well, I've never had a more gratifying one than that, and I'll enjoy your letters almost as much as having you here. But not quite."

"Oh, I shall come back to see you, before I go home to Australia."

"Then that's something very pleasant to look forward to. Enjoy your stay at Easterbrook. I hope the weather's good. With any luck, there may be some early primroses."

Randall came at eleven o'clock, earlier than he had arranged. The sun was struggling to come out, as they set off, but neither seemed to have much to say. Verity found herself remembering the last time they were in that car together, driving back from Torquay, and stopping on Dartmoor. The inescapable pain was still there in that recollection, as sharp and raw as in the beginning, and she hurriedly chose the one safe topic: "Are you still very busy?"

"Fairly, though not as bad as in January. There's quite a variety of winter ailments going round."

He sounded absent and preoccupied, and Verity gave up trying to make conversation. It was quite a short drive to the farm, and Mrs. Webber came out to greet them, and welcome Verity.

"I can't stop for lunch, I'm afraid," Randall told her. "I've had to rearrange my morning round, and must get back to Bretton now." Turning to Verity, he added: "Don't try to do too much to begin with," then got back into his car, and was off.

"That's about all we see of him just now," said Mrs. Webber resignedly. "Now, leave that case to me." She took Verity up to her room, and ran an assessing eye over her. "You certainly look as though you can do with sunshine and feeding-up. Well, we'll do our best, though I can't guarantee the sunshine."

"It's very good of you to have me," Verity began.

"Nonsense, it'll be a nice change to have more company. Nigel's at school most of the day; Bill lives nearby, but he's only just married, and we've hardly seen Randall since Christmas. When he does have a spare hour, he takes a horse out on the hills, snatches a cup of tea, and is off again. We'll be having lunch at half-past twelve, and I don't want any offers of help just yet."

She went downstairs, and Verity walked over to her window. It had a lovely view of rolling hills beyond the farm fields, very different from her usual view of Melbury village street. The room was different, too, airy and colourful, with a big bowl of snowdrops on the dressing-table.

11

WHEN Verity first came to Easterbrook Farm, she had thought that it seemed a happy house, with a friendly and serene atmosphere. She felt that even more strongly, staying there. She was accepted without fuss, and made to feel completely at home. She went to bed early the first night, slept soundly, and woke feeling much better, and even somewhat happier, Mrs Webber allowed her to help with a few of the chores. In the afternoon, she took the Labrador for a walk, and in the evenings Nigel welcomed her company with flattering enthusiasm.

It was the first break in the grey unhappiness of the last months, and the inborn gaiety of her nature began to reawaken. She had not felt like drawing for a long time, but she had packed her sketching things, thinking that they might help to fill in time in bad weather, and she would like to have some sketches of the Webber family to take back to Australia with her. The one she had already done of Nigel had been given to his mother. Now, she got them out, and drew every member of the family, and several aspects of the house and farm, with her old enjoyment.

She was sketching the front of the house on Friday afternoon, when Rowan drove up. As she got out of the car, Verity saw that she was wearing riding pants, with a brown jacket and a yellow pullover. She came over to look at her sketch.

"That's rather nice," she said approvingly, "You're looking much better. No wonder, with weather like this. I'm going for a ride. Would you like to come, too?"

Verity admitted, regretfully, that she could not ride, but decided to go with her as far as the stables. They went through the house, and Rowan stopped for a few minutes to talk to Mrs Webber. It was obvious to Verity that she was completely at home there. Out in the stable yard, she watched Rowan saddle the bay horse she had seen her riding up on the hill. She swung herself lightly into the saddle, and was off, making for the hill. As she watched her cross the first field, the pain of loss leaped out at Verity again, and she went back to her sketching, trying to concentrate all her attention on it.

Rowan stayed for tea, saying it had been a lovely day for riding, and a pity Verity could not have come with her. "If you want to learn, I'll teach you tomorrow," Nigel volunteered.

"In one day!" Rowan laughed.

"Saturday *and* Sunday. And it's getting lighter in the evenings. Have you ever been on a horse?" he asked Verity.

"A few times, when I was quite small, never since, but I'd love to learn."

239

"Then I'll take you, tomorrow morning," he promised.

Saturday was another bright day, very mild for February, so Nigel took Verity to the stables, immediately after breakfast, saddled the horse Rowan had ridden the previous day, and showed her how to mount. She felt much farther from the ground than she had expected, but the horse seemed quiet, so she was not nervous. Nigel took her rein, obviously enjoying the role of teacher, and they moved off at a sedate pace. Verity thoroughly enjoyed the next hour. The horse was well-behaved, Nigel a good, clear instructor, and Verity an apt pupil. They crossed the farm fields, and climbed the hill beyond. Sheep and young lambs were dotted all over the steep pastures, and the sea sparkled in the sunshine. Verity felt that it was good to be alive and feeling well again, on such a morning.

When they returned to the house, they had a cup of coffee with Mrs Webber.

"Verity's a natural on a horse. If I had the chance, I could make her an expert rider in six easy lessons," Nigel boasted.

"I wish you could, and I'm sure it would be entirely due to your expert teaching," Verity said, smiling.

"Don't make him more conceited than he already is," laughed his mother. "Now that both the older boys have left home, he thinks he's cock of the walk!"

Nigel disregarded this. "I'll take you again this afternoon. And you could stay here a bit longer. You won't start work until the beginning of the next week, surely?"

"You'd be *very* welcome to stay longer," Mrs Webber assured her. "But don't persuade her into doing too much, Nigel. She's still a convalescent."

Verity had enjoyed the morning so much she needed no persuading to go out again in the afternoon. When they returned to the house, Mrs Webber came to meet them.

"I've got news you won't like," she told Verity. "Randall's just rung up, to say that Colonel Nesbit is dead." Verity stared at her in stricken silence, and she added: "Randall said you were bound to be upset, that you were very attached to him. He had a second stroke early this morning, and died a few hours later. For someone of that age, it was a good way to go. He'd only had a half life since his first stroke."

"I suppose everyone would prefer a quick end," said Verity slowly. "But his was not a half life, except in a physical sense. I've never known anyone with such a lively and wide-ranging mind."

She went upstairs, and sat down on her bed. There was some truth in what Mrs Webber said, but she could not yet feel it. She had not fully realised how much she had learnt to love Colonel Nesbit, and she could not reconcile herself to the thought of never seeing him again. Her one consolation was that she would have fewer regrets when the time came to leave Westfield.

When she went down again, Mrs Webber told her that Randall had said that the funeral would probably be on Wednesday, and he would go, unless he was too busy. He had also said that he would be unable to come to the farm before Friday, so Verity might as well stay until then.

"But that's not fair to you," Verity protested. "You've been kind enough to have me for a week. I can easily arrange transport back."

"But we like having you, and Nigel will be very disappointed if you go before you have to," Mrs Webber told her. Nigel joined in, adding the prospect of more riding lessons, and it was plain to Verity that they really wanted her to stay, so she was happy to agree.

She had another riding lesson on Sunday afternoon, after going to church with the family in the morning. For the next couple of days, she helped in the house and garden, took the dog for walks, and did some sketching. Mr and

Mrs Webber intended to go to Colonel Nesbit's funeral, in a village three miles away, but Mrs Webber advised Verity not to go, as the weather had turned colder. She knew that she had made his last months pleasanter, and that attending his funeral could add nothing to that, but she wanted to see the country churchyard where he would be buried with his wife, though not with the son who had been killed in Korea.

The funeral was well attended, considering that Colonel Nesbit must have outlived many of his contemporaries. The only people Verity knew were Mr Graham, Mr and Mrs Hall, and Randall, who arrived just before the service began, and sat at the back of the church. He and Verity exchanged no conversation. While she was talking to Mrs Hall, she saw him go over to talk to his parents, and then he left, giving them both a quick greeting as he passed. Verity wondered if he still preferred to avoid her. Mrs Webber told her afterwards that he was coming to the farm on Friday afternoon, and would take her home then, if she liked, but added that she would be welcome to stay for another week-end.

The sun came out in the afternoon, so Verity decided to do some weeding in the front garden, but she had hardly started when Rowan arrived, for another ride. Verity broke off, and went to the stables with her. While she saddled the horse, Rowan asked about her riding. "If you've been out four times with Nigel, why don't you come with me now?" she suggested. "It's a lovely afternoon, and I can saddle the horse while you get ready."

Verity ran indoors, and made a quick change into pants. When she saw the horse Rowan had saddled, she felt a little dubious. "Isn't that Randall's horse?" she asked. "I've only ridden Rose-Bay so far."

"But I always ride her," laughed Rowan. "Randall won't mind your riding Turpin. He's the best trained horse in the stable, perhaps because he belongs to Randall."

Verity would have preferred the horse she was used to, but Rowan mounted, leaving her no choice, and Turpin was a beautiful horse, a glossy dark brown, and stood perfectly quiet. Verity stopped hesitating, and got into the saddle, and was soon reassured by his quiet, easy pace. They crossed the fields, climbed the hill, and rode almost to the end of the trackway.

As they turned, Rowan said, "You've good hands, and a good seat, and altogether you're a good advertisement for Nigel's tuition. Wouldn't you like to go back a bit faster?"

Hardly waiting for Verity's agreement, she started back at a canter, Verity just behind her. With increasing confidence, Verity began to enjoy the faster pace. Rowan glanced back laughing, and quickened her pace again, but then Turpin suddenly seemed to think it was a race, and shot forward, passing the other horse with ease. Verity hung on for several startled minutes, then found herself flying through the air. She landed with a thump that knocked the breath out of her, but was just struggling to her feet when Rowan reached her. She slid down from the saddle.

"Are you all right?" she asked anxiously. "I've never seen Turpin do that before."

"He probably realised he was dealing with an ignorant novice," said Verity, then began to laugh. "My behind will probably be all colours of the rainbow tomorrow, but that's the only damage."

"Well, thank goodness for that! It's my fault, but Turpin usually behaves beautifully."

"I daresay, with Randall on his back."

"Would you like me to ride him back, and you have Rose-Bay?"

Verity eyed the horse distastefully. "I'd much rather walk, but I don't like to be beaten. No, I'll ride him, but slowly, if you don't mind."

Even at an easy pace, it was an

uncomfortable ride. They unsaddled the horses and rubbed them down, and Rowan decided she hadn't time to stay for tea. Verity went in alone, determined to say nothing about her mishap, but she sat down so carefully, trying to avoid the sorest places, that Mrs. Webber wanted to know what was wrong. Verity decided she had better confess.

"You're lucky to have got off with bruises, and not a broken arm or leg," said Mrs Webber, sounding very put out. "Rowan should have let you ride the horse you know, and taken one of the others herself. She's much too fond of her own way."

Verity glanced at her curiously. "I like Rowan."

"Oh, so do I. She's a nice girl, but headstrong, and some of her ideas are altogether too modern for my taste."

There was a reserve in Mrs Webber's voice that made Verity hesitate to ask more. She had a strong feeling that the ideas which were not to her taste concerned relationships between the sexes, and her own son in particular.

She still felt stiff and sore next day, but it was a sunny afternoon, so she decided to take the dog for a final walk. It was a lovely day, milder again, with a real feel of spring in the air. She took the lane which ran downhill from the farmhouse, and stopped at a gate, to look at the lambs in the field. She pulled out her sketch-book, and began to draw some of them. They were too frisky to make easy subjects, but she became so engrossed in her drawing that she did not notice a car climbing the hill, until it braked to an abrupt, scrunching halt just beside her. She turned with a start, and Randall leaned out of the window.

"Get in," he ordered.

Verity took two or three hesitating steps towards him, her heart beating absurdly fast. "I wasn't thinking of going back to the farm yet."

"Neither am I, now," he answered, with a wide, cheerful smile. "Come on, and don't argue so much."

Verity was not sure whether she wanted to obey him or not, but when he looked at her with his old smile, she was incapable of saying no. She put the dog in the back, and got in beside Randall.

"Let's see what you were drawing." He put out a hand for her sketch book, and laughed as his eyes fell on her half-finished drawing of the field of lambs. "That's good. Perhaps it's a pity I interrupted you." He handed back the book, and began to back the car towards the gate.

"You can't possibly turn here. It's much too narrow," Verity exclaimed.

"I've known this lane for twenty-eight years," he reminded her, and then concentrated on the car. After several tight turns, when the car seemed certain to collide with the hedge, he headed safely downhill again, and Verity stopped holding her breath, and wondered where they were going, and for what purpose.

"I have something to give you," he told her. "No, it isn't from me, I'm only the messenger boy, but I'd rather not give it to you up at the house. And anyway, it's a marvellous day, and I fancy some sea air."

He said no more, and Verity sat silently beside him, wondering at this sudden change, and a little afraid, not of him but of herself. She knew that she was no good at concealing her feelings. After twisting and turning through narrow lanes, they came to a low cliff, looking west across the sea, to the North Hill. Randall stopped, fished out a small box from his pocket, and gave it to her. "Oh!" said Verity, recognising it instantly. She opened the box, and sat looking at the ring inside, struggling against tears.

"Then you know who it's from?" asked Randall.

"Yes. He showed it to me at Christmas, and told me then that he wanted me to have it some day, but I had no idea then — . I've hardly given

251

it a thought since."

"It'll have to be valued for probate some time, but Colonel Nesbit made such a point about your having it that Mr Graham thought you should have it at once, and I agreed." In spite of her efforts, a few tears trickled down Verity's cheeks. She brushed them away, as Randall added: "There's more jewellery for you, which also belonged to his wife. Did you know that?"

"No, I had no idea, but I'm not sure — "

"Don't worry. He *wanted* you to have them, and there's no one with a better right. You lightened and livened his last months. I remember his saying, soon after you started, that meals were never a bore when you brought them. He also said that you had gentle hands, imagination, and the gift of making small ordinary things funny and interesting. To have made him laugh as often as you did, that is quite something." Verity had dried her tears, but now they threatened to break out again, though for different reasons. Then Randall went on: "In spite of the fact that he could still enjoy some things, I don't think he would have wanted to linger on, month after month, let alone year after year."

"No," Verity agreed. "I saw him the morning I came here, and promised to come and see him before I went back to Australia. Of course, I knew he might not be there, but I didn't think — It was a shock, but now that I've had time to think about it, I know you're right. I often read to him. There was one poem he liked so much I know part of it by heart." She repeated the words slowly.

"*Dear beauteous Death, the jewel of the just,*
Shining nowhere but in the dark,
What mysteries do lie beyond thy dust,
Could man outlook that mark?
He that hath found some fledged bird's nest may know,
At first sight, if the bird be flown,

*But what fair well or grove he
    sings in now,
That is to him unknown."*

Their eyes met gravely, and Verity
realised that what she had missed most
of all these last three months was the
feeling of mind speaking to mind,
without need of too many words. She
looked away, not at all sure whether she
was happy to find that the link had not
been completely broken, or if that
merely made pain bite deeper.

★   ★   ★

"Did you like Mrs Marshall?" Randall
asked.

The question was so abrupt that she
turned a startled face to him. "She's
not dead, too?"

"Oh, no. I think she'll last for a good
few years yet."

"I told her that once, when she'd
said her relatives were all vultures,
sitting around, waiting to see who

would get the best pickings."

Randall said nothing, his eyes on her face, as though reading her thoughts, and Verity realised that he was still waiting for an answer to his original question. Bewildered, but obliging, she said: "I tried to like her, but I could never quite manage it. I respected her, and admired her in some ways, and sometimes felt sorry for her, but I couldn't really like her, as I did some of the others. Perhaps it was because she was so reserved, or perhaps just because she didn't like me."

"You said that before, when she had 'flu. What made you think she didn't like you?"

"How do you explain a thing like that?" Verity made a little helpless gesture with her hands. "Maybe it was because I got the job through Ralph. She's so suspicious of her family's motives. Or it might be my Australian accent. I know she didn't like that. Randall, is there some point in all this?"

"Enough to convince me that I owe

you a very humble apology. I've suspected it for some time. You really don't know that she's your great-aunt, do you?"

Verity stared at him in a staggered silence. The idea seemed fantastic enough to border on lunacy. "My great-aunt!" she exclaimed. "I don't believe it. Whatever gave you that idea?"

"She did. I think you must accept it as fact."

"But why tell you, and not me?" Verity asked, bewildered. "And why did you say nothing to me?" Then light began to dawn. "Oh, I see. She put me among the vultures. And you believed her."

She turned abruptly away from him, but Randall put his arm round her shoulders, and forced her to face him.

"I said nothing, because it was told to me in strict confidence. She said you knew all about the relationship, but hadn't realised that she had guessed, and she didn't want you to know that.

I wouldn't have believed such a tale from a stranger, but I've known Mrs Marshall all my life. You say you respected and admired her. So did I, and I thought her incapable of deliberate dishonesty. I've already apologised for believing her, and I'll do it again as often as you like."

There was pleading in his eyes and voice, and all his casual ease of manner had gone. It was not in Verity's nature not to respond. She put out both hands, her whole self shining in her eyes. He took her hands in one of his, while his other arm tightened about her shoulders.

"Let's get this tangle straightened out," he said. "Mrs Marshall said your grandmother was her only sister, that she married some kind of scapegrace, and went to Australia with him. That she only heard from her once after that, when her husband was in prison, her only child ill, and she was very short of money. Mrs Marshall said she sent her money, but never heard from her again.

When you came to work at Westfield, she wondered if you could be her sister's grand-daughter, because you were very like her, and Verity was a family name."

Verity nodded slowly. "It was my grandmother's second name, and her mother's first name." For the first time, she was beginning to credit this fantastic story.

"She said small things added up, until she was convinced, but you said nothing about the relationship, and she could think of only one reason for that, and for your coming to Westfield at all. She said she taxed Ralph with knowing about the relationship. He denied it, but finally admitted that he did know, that when he got to know you, he realised that you were her next-of-kin, and might cut out all her other relations. He agreed to introduce you to Westfield, in return for a promise to share anything you inherited from her, but you wanted to get to know her, and then you'd tell her that you'd discovered the relationship quite accidentally. He even admitted that there was a sort of understanding between you, that if you got married, it would strengthen both your claims. And of course, if she'd made no will, you would inherit everything as next-of-kin."

"Of all the beastly, squalid inventions!" interrupted Verity explosively. "Is it likely Ralph would admit all that, even if it were true? And there's not a word of truth in it. I never would have believed Mrs Marshall would invent such a pack of lies. I met Ralph quite — "

Randall put a finger on her lips, stopping her indignant flow of words. His eyes rested on hers, half-smiling, and she drew a long unsteady breath. "Let's get it quite plain. I would never have credited any of that from most people. But you've just said you'd never have believed Mrs Marshall would invent a pack of lies. Neither did I, and especially not about her own family. Some of it was obviously true, and that made me more inclined to believe it all. But since Christmas, working with you all through that 'flu, I found that I did *not* believe it any longer. It simply was not you. But neither of us had any time for explanations, and then you were ill. Now, you can tell me anything or nothing, just as you like, as long as you know that I'm very sorry that I believed any of that nonsense."

At that moment, Verity was not capable of explaining anything. She looked at him speechlessly, all her love in her eyes. He drew her close, and the loneliness and longing of these last weeks vanished beneath his lips. They kissed and kissed, pressed close, murmuring words and phrases of love, and for some time neither was capable of coherent thought.

Some time later, Verity discovered that she, too, wanted to straighten out the tangle. "If Mrs Marshall is my great-aunt, and I suppose I must believe it, if she says so," she said slowly, leaning a little back from Randall, "then I can guess why she told those lies. I know very little about my grandparents' beginnings, but enough to know that she was avenging past injuries on me."

"I really don't know much about my grandparents, except that they both came from the West Country, not even which part. Grandfather died when I was quite small, and though it's only three years since my grandmother died, she'd been living in New Zealand for a good few years before that. We wrote to each other, but about the present, not the distant past. But once, I suppose I was six or seven, I asked Gran if she'd never wanted to go back home, to see her friends and relations there. She said there'd be no welcome for her, that her parents were dead, and her only sister had quarrelled with her, and never forgiven her. She told me why. Her sister — and if she told me her name, I've forgotten it — fell in love with a young man of whom her father disapproved. There were only the two of them, their mother was dead, and this sister was their father's favourite. She wouldn't marry without his agreement, and he distrusted the man. Knowing Grandfather, I'm not surprised," Verity commented candidly. "You've probably guessed that, while this was going on, he and Gran fell in love. Maybe he'd never been in love with her sister, just thought she was a good match, I don't know. Gran wouldn't agree to marry him at first, but he said he simply could not marry her sister, and go on seeing her; that if she wouldn't marry him, he'd break the engagement and go to Australia; so they eloped, and went to Australia together."

"That seemed such a long time ago to me, I said her sister was bound to have forgiven her. Then Gran told me that she'd written to her sister once, to ask for money that she badly needed. Mrs Marshall told you that she'd sent it, but she didn't say that her response to her sister's letter was to put a cheque in an envelope, and send it without one friendly word. Gran said it seemed like a slap in the face, and she realised that she would never be forgiven. It seemed so vindictive to me, I've never forgotten it. Obviously, she meant me to pay for what Gran did to her, but to carry a desire for revenge down to the third generation, I can't understand that."

"No quarrels quite so bitter as family quarrels," said Randall slowly. "I should have thought of that. I jump to conclusions too quickly. I only hope I don't in my work." How typical of Randall to think on those lines, even at that moment, Verity thought. Answering laughter gleamed in his eyes. "It's not just a job, but a whole way of life, as you know, but at least you are warned." Verity knew that his mind had jumped to the thought in hers, without a word spoken, and she drew a long breath of unalloyed happiness. "You are going to marry me, I hope?" he added.

The thought of Rowan came into her mind, for the first time since she had seen Randall. "But what about Rowan?" she asked. "I thought — ." His eyebrows shot up in unfeigned surprise. "Well, what was I to think?" she demanded, in exasperated tones. "The temperature dropped below freezing, just at the exact time she came here. She's beautiful, and I'm not. What would any girl think?"

"She's dazzlingly beautiful," he mocked. "I'm sorry, darling, I'd never even noticed the coincidence of time. I like Rowan, but I don't happen to love her. We wouldn't suit, anyway. I like a lasting relationship, one that has plenty of time to grow." Verity was sure that Rowan found Randall very attractive, and she wondered a little about that last comment. But then he went on: "You're the only girl I've ever wanted to marry, but I thought we had plenty of time. And then everything went wrong. Will you forgive me, and marry me?"

"Of course." Verity's eyes spoke much more eloquently than her words, and their lips met in a long kiss. Some time later, she said: "There's something else you don't know; nor Mrs Marshall, apparently. All that about my being next-of-kin, I'm not. When Gran wrote to her sister, Mother was presumably her only child, but she had a son, ten years younger. He's alive and flourishing, in New Zealand. That's why Gran went to live there, after Mother died. So he's Mrs Marshall's next-of-kin, and he has three sons."

"In the unlikely event of her not having made a will, you'd get your mother's share. But does it matter now?"

"I don't like being put among the vultures. If she'd only told me that she thought we were related, I'd have been delighted to find some family here. I can't understand how anyone could cherish resentment and bitterness for so long. I'm beginning to think she's got the sort of relations she deserves."

"From you, that's an unexpectedly uncharitable remark," Randall observed, smiling gently. "She could have had a lot of pleasure from finding a new niece. She has definitely been her own worst enemy."

"She must have guessed who I was from the beginning," said Verity slowly, "and bided her time, knowing that I was friendly with Ralph, and then with you, until she thought I was probably in love with one of you. Not being sure which, she told a variation of the story to each of you, probably told Ralph she'd cut him out of her will, unless he dropped me like a hot cake, which he did. Yet Grandfather really did her a good turn when he jilted her. Oh, that wasn't his motive, but *she'd* soon have been *miserable* with him. Gran was quite different, very easy-going, happy under most circumstances."

"You must be rather like her. Forget them all." Randall drew his finger gently over the contours of her face. "Verity, Verity, Verity," he repeated softly, and somehow she liked it better than any number of endearments and protestations. She leaned against him, still a little dazed by happiness. "Isn't it strange, there are any number of attractive, likeable, and amusing girls in the world, but only one who just fits you, like putting your hand in your own glove?"

"You won't always feel like that."

"Then I'll settle for feeling like that part of the time! That's good enough for me. Let's get married soon, and I'll take you to look at England in spring."

"Lovely!" But then Verity paused. "I don't know whether my father will want to come for my wedding. If he does, I'd have to wait."

"Fair enough, providing he doesn't expect us to wait too long. Write to him straight away."

Reminded of the rest of the world, she sat up and looked at her watch. "Randall, your mother will be wondering what's happened to me! I only went out for a middling walk."

"All right, we'll go back. She'll be delighted with the news."

Verity picked up the small leather box. "When Colonel Nesbit showed me this ring, at Christmas, he suggested that I might wear it as an engagement ring. I'd like to. Would you mind?"

"At Christmas," he repeated, and from the quick glance of his eyes she knew that he guessed how she had felt about that. "No, I wouldn't mind. I'll buy you something else instead of a ring, perhaps some other jewellery." Then sudden laughter came into his eyes. "Now that you've learnt to ride, I could buy you a horse of your own. What colour are the bruises?"

"All colours of the rainbow. Rowan told you?"

"It just seeped out, but I told her what I thought about it, putting a beginner on Turpin. And then I suppose *she* encouraged you to canter? Why do you think I called him Turpin?" Verity looked blank, and he laughed again. "I keep forgetting that you were brought up on a different set of legends, and may be more familiar with Ned Kelly. Dick Turpin's horse was reputed to show a clean pair of heels to every other horse in England. Turpin's safe enough, at a walk, but give him his head, and he takes some holding. I'd hoped to take you for a ride this evening, but I think we'd better postpone it. All right, I'll take you back for tea — in five minutes!"

THE END

WITH SOMEBODY ELSE
Theresa Charles

Rosamond sets off for Cornwall with Hugo to meet his family, blissfully unaware of the shocks in store for her.

A SUMMER FOR STRANGERS
Claire Hamilton

Because she had lost her job, her flat and she had no money, Tabitha agreed to pose as Adam's future wife although she believed the scheme to be deceitful and cruel.

VILLA OF SINGING WATER
Angela Petron

The disquieting incidents that occurred at the Vatican and the Colosseum did not trouble Jan at first, but then they became increasingly unpleasant and alarming.

DOCTOR NAPIER'S NURSE
Pauline Ash

When cousins Midge and Derry are entered as probationer nurses on the same day but at different hospitals they agree to exchange identities.

A GIRL LIKE JULIE
Louise Ellis

Caroline absolutely adored Hugh Barrington, but then Julie Crane came into their lives. Julie was the kind of girl who attracts men without even trying.

COUNTRY DOCTOR
Paula Lindsay

When Evan Richmond bought a practice in a remote country village he did not realise that a casual encounter would lead to the loss of his heart.

ENCORE
Helga Moray

Craig and Janet realise that their true happiness lies with each other, but it is only under traumatic circumstances that they can be reunited.

NICOLETTE
Ivy Preston

When Grant Alston came back into her life, Nicolette was faced with a dilemma. Should she follow the path of duty or the path of love?

THE GOLDEN PUMA
Margaret Way

Catherine's time was spent looking after her father's Queensland farm. But what life was there without David, who wasn't interested in her?

HOSPITAL BY THE LAKE
Anne Durham

Nurse Marguerite Ingleby was always ready to become personally involved with her patients, to the despair of Brian Field, the Senior Surgical Registrar, who loved her.

VALLEY OF CONFLICT
David Farrell

Isolated in a hostel in the French Alps, Ann Russell sees her fiancé being seduced by a young girl. Then comes the avalanche that imperils their lives.

NURSE'S CHOICE
Peggy Gaddis

A proposal of marriage from the incredibly handsome and wealthy Reagan was enough to upset any girl — and Brooke Martin was no exception.

A DANGEROUS MAN
Anne Goring

Photographer Polly Burton was on safari in Mombasa when she met enigmatic Leon Hammond. But unpredictability was the name of the game where Leon was concerned.

PRECIOUS INHERITANCE
Joan Moules

Karen's new life working for an authoress took her from Sussex to a foreign airstrip and a kidnapping; to a real life adventure as gripping as any in the books she typed.

VISION OF LOVE
Grace Richmond

When Kathy takes over the rundown country kennels she finds Alec Stinton, a local vet, very helpful. But their friendship arouses bitter jealousy and a tragedy seems inevitable.

HEART OF ICE
Marie Sidney

How was January to know that not only would the warmth of the Swiss people thaw out her frozen heart, but that she too would play her part in helping someone to live again?

LUCKY IN LOVE
Margaret Wood

Companion-secretary to wealthy gambler Laura Duxford, who lived in Monaco, seemed to Melanie a fabulous job. Especially as Melanie had already lost her heart to Laura's son, Julian.

NURSE TO PRINCESS JASMINE
Lilian Woodward

Nick's surgeon brother, Tom, performs an operation on an Arabian princess, and she invites Tom, Nick and his fiancé to Omander, where a web of deceit and intrigue closes about them.

THE WAYWARD HEART
Eileen Barry
Disaster-prone Katherine's nickname was 'Kate Calamity', but her boss went too far with an outrageous proposal, which because of her latest disaster, she could not refuse.

FOUR WEEKS IN WINTER
Jane Donnelly
Tessa wasn't looking forward to meeting Paul Mellor again — she had made a fool of herself over him once before. But was Orme Jared's solution to her problem likely to be the right one?

SURGERY BY THE SEA
Sheila Douglas
Medical student Meg hadn't really wanted to go and work with a G.P. on the Welsh coast although the job had its compensations. But Owen Roberts was certainly not one of them!

HEAVEN IS HIGH
Anne Hampson
The new heir to the Manor of Marbeck had been found. But it was rather unfortunate that when he arrived unexpectedly he found an uninvited guest, complete with stetson and high boots.

LOVE WILL COME
Sarah Devon
June Baker's boss was not really her idea of her ideal man, but when she went from third typist to boss's secretary overnight she began to change her mind.

ESCAPE TO ROMANCE
Kay Winchester
Oliver and Jean first met on Swale Island. They were both trying to begin their lives afresh, but neither had bargained for complications from the past.

CASTLE IN THE SUN
Cora Mayne

Emma's invalid sister, Kym, needed a warm climate, and Emma jumped at the chance of a job on a Mediterranean island. But Emma soon finds that intrigues and hazards lurk on the sunlit isle.

BEWARE OF LOVE
Kay Winchester

Carol Brampton resumes her nursing career when her family is killed in a car accident. With Dr. Patrick Farrell she begins to pick up the pieces of her life, but is bitterly hurt when insinuations are made about her to Patrick.

DARLING REBEL
Sarah Devon

When Jason Farradale's secretary met with an accident, her glamorous stand-in was quite unable to deal with one problem in particular.

THE PRICE OF PARADISE
Jane Arbor

It was a shock to Fern to meet her estranged husband on an island in the middle of the Indian Ocean, but to discover that her father had engineered it puzzled Fern. What did he hope to achieve?

DOCTOR IN PLASTER
Lisa Cooper

When Dr. Scott Sutcliffe is injured, Nurse Caroline Hurst has to cope with a very demanding private case. But when she realises her exasperating patient has stolen her heart, how can Caroline possibly stay?

A TOUCH OF HONEY
Lucy Gillen

Before she took the job as secretary to author Robert Dean, Cadie had heard how charming he was, but that wasn't her first impression at all.

ROMANTIC LEGACY
Cora Mayne

As kennelmaid to the Armstrongs, Ann Brown, had no idea that she would become the central figure in a web of mystery and intrigue.

THE RELENTLESS TIDE
Jill Murray

Steve Palmer shared Nurse Marie Blane's love of the sea and small boats. Marie's other passion was her step-brother. But when danger threatened who should she turn to — her step-brother or the man who stirred emotions in her heart?

ROMANCE IN NORWAY
Cora Mayne

Nancy Crawford hopes that her visit to Norway will help her to start life again. She certainly finds many surprises there, including unexpected happiness.

SHADOW DANCE
Margaret Way

When Carl Danning sent her to interview Richard Kauffman, Alix was far from pleased — but the assignment led her to help Richard repair the situation between him and his ex-wife.

WHITE HIBISCUS
Rosemary Pollock

'A boring English model with dubious morals,' was how Count Paul Santana Demajo described Emma. But what about the Count's morals, and who is Marianne?

STARS THROUGH THE MIST
Betty Neels

Secretly in love with Gerard van Doordninck, Deborah should have been thrilled when he asked her to marry him. But he only wanted a wife for practical not romantic reasons.